HAVE YOU SEEN THIS GIRL

ALSO BY NITA TYNDALL

Who I Was with Her

Nothing Sung and Nothing Spoken

HAVE YOU SEEN THIS GIRL

Nita Tyndall

HARPER TEEN
An Imprint of HarperCollins*Publishers*

HarperTeen is an imprint of HarperCollins Publishers

 For information address HarperCollins Children's Books, a division of HarperCollins Publishers, 195 Broadway, New York, NY 10007.
www.epicreads.com

Library of Congress Control Number: 2023943347
ISBN 978-0-06-330588-5

Typography by Julia Feingold

24 25 26 27 28 LBC 5 4 3 2 1
First Edition

For Kate, my "home friend,"
and for Hannah, my home.

Chapter One

MY FATHER didn't murder June Hargrove. By the time she was killed, he was already in prison for the murders of five other girls. No one in their right mind would think he had anything to do with killing June Hargrove.

But then her body was found in the same lake he used to dump his victims in, and—well. This town needs someone to blame, and while they can't point a finger at him, they can sure as hell point one at me.

June Hargrove is found in Cardinal Lake on a rainy Friday afternoon a little less than a week after she disappeared. Half the town stands on the banks and watches as she's recovered.

I stand at the back. No one wants me here, the living reminder of what my father did, but once I heard she'd been found in the lake, I had to know.

I need to see her. Need to see her head, because then—then I'll know.

We all hold our breaths as June's father steps forward to identify her body. Girl like that goes missing, it becomes a town affair. We can pretend she ran away all we want, and I know the Hargroves would probably have preferred that, but in a town that's had this happen before, the first place a lot of people's minds are going to go is to my dad and what he did.

I keep my hood up. Shoulders hunched. But anyone who glances my way, who looks too long, will know it's me. The murderer's kid.

If I'd been born a boy, I would've been called a bastard. But they all see me as a girl, so I'm just a bitch.

I shove my hands deeper into my pockets and sneak off to the side for a better view. I'm itching for a cigarette, but that'll just draw more attention.

But then I bump right into Mrs. Crenshaw, and her mouth twists down in recognition. She opens it to say something, but whatever she was going to say is drowned out by Mrs. Hargrove's wailing, all the confirmation we need that it was June who's been pulled from the lake.

Still. Mrs. Crenshaw has a set of lungs on her, too, and her shouting my full name doesn't go unnoticed by Sheriff Kepler, even if his men are busy zipping up June into a body bag.

I need to go. I know that. But I need to see her head first, so I push through the crowd rather than away from it.

It doesn't matter. I can't see anything. The sheriff's men stand in a line at the front, blocking June's body from view. All

I can see is Sheriff Kepler, his eyes scanning the crowd until they finally meet mine.

I turn and run.

The TV's on when I get home. Gram's got her slippers on, and the Reverend Billy Engel is blaring from the TV set. Never mind it's a rerun; never mind Billy Engel's been dead for three years. His message of Our Lord is always relevant.

"They find her?" she asks.

"Yeah." I kick off my shoes by the door. "Yeah. They found her."

"Yer daddy didn't do it."

"I know," I say, like I need her to remind me, but there's a twist in my gut all the same. "But that means someone did."

"They'll catch him," she says, not taking her eyes off the TV.

They won't. They didn't catch Dad for years.

Then again. June Hargrove is a white, pretty girl from a family on the nicer side of town. This might get solved faster than Dad's killings ever did.

"Think there'll be a funeral?"

"I dunno. Ain't like I'll go, anyway," I say. I settle on the couch next to her. She smells like cigarette smoke and too much White Diamonds perfume.

"You should go pay your respects."

"She's not gonna feel 'em," I say. "Besides. No one wants me there."

Gram nods. "Did you know her?"

"Not well," I say. We had three classes together, but that doesn't mean much. I knew her in the same way I know most of my classmates—because we've all gone to the same schools together since kindergarten.

"Well. It's a shame," Gram says, and she turns up the volume on the TV.

It's always a shame when girls die too young. I don't need her to tell me that.

LAUREN O'MALLEY
ALICIA GRAVES
MELISSA WAGNER
DAWN SCHAEFER
SAMANTHA MARKHAM

These are the girls my father killed, the girls who used to call my name at night, whose voices I used to hear in my ears.

LAUREN O'MALLEY
ALICIA GRAVES
MELISSA WAGNER
DAWN SCHAEFER
SAMANTHA MARKHAM
~~JUNE HARGROVE~~

He didn't. I know he didn't. He had nothing to do with her death.

But I couldn't see her head, so I don't know for sure.

"Hello. This is a prepaid collect call from Dennis Crane, an inmate at North Carolina Central Prison. This call is subject to recording and monitoring. To accept this call, press one."

Ten thirty. Right on time.

I shut the door to my bedroom and sit with the phone to my ear. This is the only reason we have a landline anymore. Gram's asleep in front of the TV, which is fine.

She hates when he calls. She never talks to him.

Truth told, I don't know why I do. I guess it's just habit for both of us.

But I wouldn't miss a chance to talk to him today. I didn't tell him when June Hargrove went missing less than a week ago, praying, like everyone else in this town, that she'd simply run off, but now I know. Now I have to bring it up.

I sit cross-legged on my bed, pick at the loose thread in the toe of my sock, make a mental note to pick up a new pack at the grocery store.

"Hey, Daddy," I say.

"Sid."

I swallow. I know I should say something more. These calls are expensive, and it's a waste if we don't talk.

And I have to ask him.

"Did . . . did you hear about June Hargrove?" I ask.

My mouth is like paste. There's silence on the other end of the line.

And then my father does something he's never done in all the years we've been doing these phone calls.

He hangs up.

I go for a ride. Gram's still asleep when I leave my bedroom, pull on my shoes, and put my hood up. Don't bother slapping a piece of reflective tape to my back; if someone runs me over, it's their problem.

I don't know where I'm riding to. I skid down our gravel driveway, through the woods, down the almost mile-long path it takes to get to the road from our trailer.

Better no one knows we live back here. Gram's tried to keep it hidden from the town. I moved in with her when I was thirteen. We changed our last names, and we tried to distance ourselves from what he'd done.

It doesn't matter. Everyone looks at me and only sees the murderer's daughter. I can change my appearance, my name all I want. What he's done still sticks to me, haunts me like his victims do.

I pedal harder. Down back roads, not sure where I'm heading until June Hargrove's face pops up in front of me so suddenly I lose my balance and go tumbling into a ditch.

Fuck. My hands and knees sting, I'm spitting dirt out of my mouth, and I look up and she's still there.

I forgot about that fucking billboard.

It's at least twenty feet high, June's senior portrait plastered all over it, her teeth as tall as my body. And in big black letters:

HAVE YOU SEEN THIS GIRL?

Except some of the letters are peeling off, so it almost reads like SEE THIS GIRL.

See her?

Do you see her?

She's pretty and young and white, and she didn't deserve to die, and—

My father hung up on me.

When I asked him about June. He hung up.

And I know, I *know* he didn't do it. He couldn't have. Logically, there's no way he could have.

But June Hargrove's face is staring down at me from that fucking billboard and all I can think is, if he didn't do it—

Who did?

June's face follows me to the QuikMart, a poster on a telephone pole, a sign in a storefront. Have You Seen This Girl?

Occasionally they change. Occasionally it's Have You Seen

Me?, June herself reaching out and pleading with us to find her.

I didn't see her. Today. I didn't see her body and I don't know if her head was shaved like the rest of the girls my father killed. Like mine.

My hood flies back as I pull into the parking lot of the Quik-Mart, exposing my buzzed scalp to the rain. Freud would have a fucking field day with this. With my head being like theirs, fuzz between my fingers.

But it's different. I chose to do this. I *chose.*

And I'm not fully a girl, anyway. I'm just Sid, whose father is a murderer, whose head is shaved, who rides a bike at eleven at night even though a girl just got killed.

I park my bike at the front of the store, in front of the neon sign advertising this week's winning lottery numbers. Don't bother locking it because no one's around to steal it, anyway; there's just the one truck in the parking lot and I know exactly who that belongs to.

I pull my hood back up as I enter the store. It doesn't do any good.

"Eyyy, Sid the Kid."

"Terry," I say, looking up at him.

Terry Pritchard fixes me with a grin, greasy hair falling over his pale face. I can see the dirt under his nails from here. He's built like a beanpole, long and lanky and too skinny. He's only two years older than me, his brother, Johnny, nine years older than him. He would've been a junior when I was a freshman if he hadn't dropped out of high school.

Not that I can blame him for that. I can blame him for being a creep, though. I'm not his type, but I've seen girls from my school in here sometimes, when their boyfriends talk them into buying beer because "Scary Terry won't say no to you." Watched him leer down enough shirts to know exactly what kind of person he is.

I shuffle to the back of the store. I can still feel Terry watching me, but I don't shiver. Don't show any sign of disgust. He feeds on it like a parasite.

My face is perfectly neutral when I return to the counter a few minutes later with a bag of salt-and-vinegar chips for me and a bag of barbecue pork rinds for Gram. I don't look at Terry as I slide the items across the counter.

Instead I look at June. Even here I can't escape her, escape the way she stares out at me from a grainy black-and-white photo taped on the outside of an old Folgers coffee can. There's a slit in the lid for people to put change in, like their quarters would've helped her get found.

Wonder what'll happen to all that loose change, now she's dead. Terry'll probably pocket it.

Have You Seen Me?

"Pack of Morleys, too," I say, mouth dry as I finally turn my attention toward Terry.

"Already rung 'em up," he says. "I know what you like, Sid."

I make eye contact with him. He looks deliberately down at June on the coffee can, then back up at me.

"So," he says. "Did he do it?"

There's no need to clarify which *he* he means.

"He's up in prison, Terry. Didn't think you were born yesterday," I say.

Terry laughs. It's a harsh, ugly bark. I go to take my plastic bag from him, but he holds it out of my reach, forces me to lean in.

"Did you do it?" he asks, eyes shining and voice low. "Sid the Killer's Kid, huh? Did you?"

He dangles it closer and I snatch the plastic bag out of his hand and almost run to the door, that fucking barking laugh following me all the way out.

It's still raining on the way home, so by the time I get back, my legs are covered in mud and my hoodie sticks to me like a second skin. The cigarettes are tucked in my sports bra so they don't get wet, and at least I could turn my back when I tucked them in so Terry couldn't see. Chips and pork rinds I'm not too worried about.

Gram's still asleep in front of the TV, Billy Engel still going on about eternal damnation. I set her bag of pork rinds on the counter and grab my chips and head down the hall to my room.

Dad hung up on me. June Hargrove's body was found floating in the lake this afternoon, and Dad hung up on me when I asked him about it.

I know he couldn't have done it. I know that.

There was doubt when he was initially arrested, a lot of people saying Sheriff Kepler just wanted to make an arrest on a case to prove himself. There was doubt for a long, long time, because how could one man not get caught after five years? He had to have had an accomplice, people thought.

But then my dad confessed, and that doubt went away. For the town, anyway. For Gram.

It should have gone away for me, but what child wants to believe their father is a murderer? I clung to that theory, that scrap, even after he insisted that he'd acted alone.

I've buried that doubt as deep as I can, but sometimes it still comes creeping out. Like now.

I should feel sad that June's gone. I should feel torn up that a girl is dead, but all I can feel is fear that my father had something to do with it. That doubt creeping back in—what if he actually did have an accomplice? What if someone else helped him and never got caught, and they're back now to finish what he started, ten years after the first murders?

Worse, what if they're doing it because he told them to? What if this is still his idea?

Did he do it?

Did you do it?

Fuck.

I was seven when the first girls went missing, thirteen when Dad was arrested. Too young to have suspicion pointed at me then, but now—

I put a pillow over my face and scream until I don't have a voice left, until I can't say anything.

Just like June.

Chapter Two

JUNE FOLLOWS me to school Monday. It's impossible to escape her there. Everyone is talking about her, her name floating through whispers on the air. She's more present now than she has been for the past week, where we've all been skirting around her absence, because acknowledging it means acknowledging something bad might have happened to her. It's been easy to pretend—she's just sick, she ran away.

Now, though? Now she's all anyone can talk about.

Anyone except me.

Who killed June Hargrove?

I heard she drowned/I heard she was stabbed/I heard/I heard/I heard—

Did he do it?

Did you *do it?*

During homeroom I overhear Sally Louise Kepler whisper something to Lilah Crenshaw about the funeral. Lilah shushes her when she realizes I'm listening.

She doesn't need to worry. I'm not going.

Our teachers don't even bother trying to stop anyone from gossiping. They're gray-faced and red-eyed. June's seat in second-period English is empty. It's been empty almost since the start of the semester, but we've all been hoping she'll come back and fill it.

Guess not.

Half of the girls in my English class have to be excused because they can't stop crying. They leave for the bathroom in groups, clutching each other's arms. At one point, Sally Louise and I are the only ones sitting there, besides the boys.

The boys would cry, too, but they don't. Can't. Aren't allowed to.

I sit in the back and itch for a cigarette.

By lunch it's clear we're not going to get anything done. Principal Johnston declares it a half day in memory of June and adds if anyone wants details on the funeral to see Mrs. Hill.

We all head out to the parking lot. Most girls still walk in packs. Mr. Wolf was the last one to see her leave school around four. She'd stayed late to ask about her chemistry grade.

They found her car a few blocks from the school, pulled over on the side of the road. The doors were unlocked.

They're running all the usual tests—on the car, on her body. We don't really know how she died, not yet.

God, I hope she wasn't strangled. I hope her head wasn't shaved.

The doubt that my father wasn't involved rears its head now even stronger.

Who kills a girl like June Hargrove?

I know who does. He raised me.

But no one cared about Dad's victims until the third girl went missing, until they thought there might be a larger pattern. June got more attention from the start because of him, because this town's already been through hell once. Because it's already seen what happens to girls who go missing in Cardinal Creek.

It starts raining again as I bike home, passing a guy taking down some of June's missing posters.

Something ugly twists in my stomach when I realize it's Terry. He catches my eye as I bike past, giving me a grin.

"Killer," he mouths, then laughs.

Someone is sitting in June's seat.

A girl is sitting in June's seat.

Time seems to slow down. The bell rings for the start of second period and half of us are still standing, staring at this girl who's sitting in June Hargrove's seat. Even Mrs. Hill seems shocked by her.

But none of us have ever seen her before, and she's sitting in June's seat. How are we not supposed to stare?

Mrs. Hill finally regains some control, motioning for all of us to take our own seats. We do, but the whispers just keep coming.

Who is she?

Why is she sitting there?

Doesn't she know?

Doesn't she know whose seat that is?

Who is she?

To her credit, the girl doesn't look at any of us. She keeps her head down and her nose buried in her copy of *Jane Eyre*, which we were supposed to continue discussing today. Mrs. Hill partnered us up at the beginning of the semester.

June was my partner. Was supposed to be. But she was only here for two days before she disappeared, so we barely made it past the first chapter. Mrs. Hill hasn't bothered to put me with anyone else's group—hoping, I think, that June would come back.

Or hoping to spare both of us the awkwardness of trying to place me in a group when no one wants to work with me.

"Class, this is Mavis Hastings. She'll be joining us for the rest of the semester," Mrs. Hill says, in that no-nonsense tone that doesn't invite any questions.

I sit right behind her. I sat right behind June, too, though that never felt like anything until her seat was empty.

Mavis keeps her head down. I don't blame her.

We make our way through *Jane Eyre*, all of our heads bowed, not daring to glance around at each other, at the girl in June's seat.

June's seat that's already filled by someone else when her funeral is tonight.

Mrs. Hill launches into her analysis of the chapters we're supposed to have read, and I sneak a glance at the back of Mavis's head. Her haircut is uneven, like she might have done it herself.

She's so different from June. They're both white teenage girls, but June's hair was long and straight and dark where Mavis's is short and curly and dirty blond; June was organized and prepared in every class I ever had with her, and I can see from here this girl's backpack is a stuffed mess. June always sat straight up, like she was going to be graded on her posture, too, and Mavis is hunched over her desk.

June had freckles. I can't tell if this girl does, too.

Someone starts sniffling, breaking me out of my thoughts. I crane my neck to see who, but then it doesn't matter, because it's set off half the class again.

Mavis hunches farther down in her seat.

"Maybe we'll skip the part about Helen," Mrs. Hill says suddenly, and flips forward in her book.

Christ, what did I miss?

I hastily pull my battered library copy out of my bag and flip to the chapter we were supposed to read, skimming the pages, until my eyes catch on the name Helen, and then a few pages later—

Oh. Fuck. No wonder everyone is crying. June's funeral is today; how are we supposed to read about another dead girl?

"Mrs. Hill?"

I look around for the voice. It's Mavis, slamming her book shut. "Can I . . . can I be excused? Please?"

Mrs. Hill looks startled. Mavis didn't know June; there's no reason for her to be upset, even if the girls around her are—unless she already knows. Or could be she's just upset because everyone's acting so weird around her. I wonder what this must look like for her, her first day here and everyone around her won't stop crying or whispering.

If I were her, I'd never come back after that.

"Of—of course," she says, and Mavis packs up her things and almost runs out the door, her books clutched to her chest.

The sniffling continues. Mrs. Hill tries to regain control, but it's useless. No one's paying attention to *Jane Eyre*, not when there's real drama happening in front of us. She eventually lets us read in silence until the bell rings.

I'm out of my seat the second the bell goes off. We have an hour for lunch, and I plan to spend that hour away from everyone else, hiding under the bleachers and smoking a cigarette.

Before June went missing, we could leave during lunch. Not anymore. Used to seniors and juniors could drive to the local Cook Out, eat and smoke and just get the hell out of here. But three days after she went missing, the principal decided we had to stay on campus. The boys were angry. We could hear them muttering under their breath—*not like we're stupid enough to get killed.*

Like it's June's fault she left school after dark.

But that's what you get when you're a girl.

My back's against the metal post of the bleachers, and a cigarette is between my fingers. I keep my hood up, glance around every so often to make sure no one is looking.

I should go to the funeral. Shouldn't I? Pay my respects. That's what Gram would want.

And my dad didn't kill her. And I did know her. And I have every right to grieve with the rest of this fucking town.

She's one girl. It's awful, but she's one girl who got killed and it's not like it was before.

But that doubt creeps in all the same.

"Can I sit?"

I jump, open my eyes. There's a shadow falling over me and I look up to see Mavis, arms crossed over her chest, gnawing on her lower lip.

I keep smoking.

"Look, everyone's fucking staring at me and I need to hide and I'm sorry you're here, but I need to be alone so can I just . . . sit?"

It takes me a minute to find my voice. "Yeah. Yeah, sure."

Mavis sits down next to me, closing her own eyes. I finish my cigarette and grind it into the dirt.

"Is it always like this whenever someone new moves here?" she asks. I look up. She's got her arms wrapped around her knees, her chin buried in them. "I feel like a specimen."

"Not always," I say. "Usually it's worse." I wonder if she's heard about what happened to June. If she knows she'd been sitting in a seat that belonged to a dead girl.

She looks at me like she can't tell if I'm joking or not before she cracks a smile. "Good one." She picks at a stray thread on her blue sweatshirt. She looks miserable.

I should tell her. She should know, at least, why everyone's acting so weird.

"It's . . . it really isn't like this normally," I say. "But—but a girl just died. June. And that was her seat."

"Oh," Mavis says. "Oh, shit, I heard people talking about that when we bought groceries last night, but I didn't think she—shit."

My heart quickens. If she heard someone in town talking about June Hargrove—

What has she heard about me?

"Thanks—for telling me. I was going to go the rest of the day thinking it was me," Mavis says, and she sounds sarcastic, but there's something under that, too. A note of fear.

"It could still be you," I say, trying again to joke. "We don't get new people that often."

"I didn't mean just being new," she says, but she doesn't elaborate. She goes back to picking at the thread on her sweatshirt before seeming to realize she's doing it and stopping.

"What did you mean?" I finally ask, and she sighs.

"Doesn't matter. I don't know you, anyway, and the less you know, the better."

"What if I want to know you?"

I don't know what makes me say it. Maybe it's something about the way she doesn't belong here, just like I don't.

She smirks. "You could tell me your name first."

"Sid."

"That short for anything?"

I shake my head, quick. "No. Just Sid." I pull another cigarette out of the pack, even though I should be trying to quit, even though they're expensive and I should be trying to save them. "Want one?"

Mavis shakes her head. "No."

"Mind if I . . . ?"

"Yeah," she says. "I mind."

I put the cigarette back in the pack, stuff it into my hoodie pocket.

"How'd she die?" Mavis asks after a minute, and I look at her. "June," she clarifies, like she needs to, like it's not clear who she's asking about.

"She—we think she was killed," I say, and Mavis's face pales, like she hadn't expected me to say that, like she had expected a car crash or some sort of accident or any of the other multitude of things that kill teenage girls.

The fear that she overheard someone in town talking about me dissipates, just a little. If she didn't know June was murdered, she wouldn't have heard about my dad.

"Shit," she says. "Do they know who did it?"

"Not yet," I say. I really am itching for a cigarette now. "They just found her body."

"Oh," she says. "Does that kind of thing happen here a lot?"

It feels like such a weird question to ask, and it immediately has me on guard. I pull back.

"No," I say shortly. "No, not really. Town's small. We don't . . . we don't get a lot of crime." I refuse to think about my dad. Or the possibility that June's murder has anything to do with him. It was a one-off. That's all it can be.

But I didn't see her head. I didn't see it, so I can't be sure.

"That's good, at least," she says. Then, "Hey. Would you want to hang out after school? You can show me around."

I can't have heard her right. "What?"

"Do you want to hang out?" she asks. She looks away. "Or not, if you're busy—"

"I'm not busy," I say. "I might stop by June's funeral, but after that, I'm free."

It feels weird, saying it. Like her funeral is a social engagement and not us mourning for a dead girl. Then again, the whole town's going to treat it like a social engagement, so . . .

"Right. Funeral," Mavis says. "Did you know her?"

"Not well, beyond class," I say. "But the whole town is going."

"Why?"

"Why didn't I know June better?"

"No. Why is the whole town going to her funeral?"

"You're not from a small town, are you?"

She shakes her head again. "Chicago."

"Oh. So you . . . you won't get it."

She leans back on her hands, stares at me. "Try me."

I'm about to, about to tell her what it's like in this small fucking town where everyone knows everyone and their business, when the bell rings. Mavis stands up first, brushing dust off the back of her jeans. I stand, too, pulling out a cigarette but not lighting it.

"Here," she says, handing me her phone. "Text me when you're done with the funeral. We could—I dunno. Where's good to eat around here?"

I type my number in and hand her phone back to her. My own buzzes with a text—from her so that I'll have her number, I'm sure.

I shrug. "I'll show you. Meet me at the diner on Main?"

Mavis scoffs. "You have a Main Street," she says, then waves as we split and head to our separate classes.

I look down at my phone. The message she sent was:

hey, it's mavis <3

I think about that little heart all through civics. About her. This girl from Chicago who doesn't know me, or my dad, or what he's done.

I might actually have a chance at . . . something.

But then I hear Alison Woods and Lilah Crenshaw snickering behind me, and when I twist around, Lilah catches my eye and smirks, and my stomach sinks.

I might actually have a chance—as long as someone doesn't tell Mavis who I am first.

Chapter Three

I MAKE it all the way to the parking lot of the funeral home before deciding I'm not going in. The lot is so full, people are parked all the way down the street. I joked with Mavis that everyone was going to be here, but I think part of me didn't expect all these people to actually show up.

And I can't stop thinking about the question from Mavis and Gram about if I knew June or not. I really didn't beyond occasionally asking her what the homework was. She was friends with Craig Hutchens and Savannah Baunach and a whole other pack of people she knew from cheerleading. We didn't really have a reason to talk.

She knew who my dad was, of course. But at least she never brought it up to me.

Besides. I'm not going to get answers at her funeral. It's closed casket, so I've heard. Anyone coming to see the murdered girl's body missed their chance.

I watch as Sally Louise, the sheriff's daughter, gets out of her car and leans on her boyfriend. Once upon a time I could have asked her about the autopsy reports. She might have even told me what I needed to know.

Once upon a time Sally Louise was my best friend, all the way up until we were thirteen. All the way up until her dad became the sheriff and decided he needed to be the one who solved what had happened to the missing girls back in 2008. All the way up until he showed up at my door a few months before my birthday and asked if my father was home.

We stopped being friends when her dad arrested mine. Middle-school friendships are tenuous enough. Ours once barely survived a fight at a sleepover. We couldn't survive something worse than that.

We haven't really spoken since.

She catches my eye as she walks up the stairs. My hood is up, but her mouth twists in recognition all the same.

Her boyfriend turns, too, just to see who she's staring at. But she lays her hand on his arm and he turns back around.

She doesn't, though. She keeps glancing back my way as she goes into the building, and I can still feel her eyes on me long after she's gone.

No. I can't go in there. If I go in there, it won't just be Sally Louise looking at me, but the whole town. I don't need that. June doesn't need that, the living reminder of what my father has done.

Her body is reminder enough.

◆ ◆ ◆

No one else is in the diner when I arrive, waiting for Mavis. I texted to let her know I'd be earlier than we planned since I didn't go to the funeral. I'm relieved the diner is open; I hadn't even considered it might be closed for the funeral. But Jackson Miller and his father, Darius, are still behind the counter, Jackson leaning on it and staring, bored, at the door.

He nods at me as I sit down. We've had a few classes together but never really spoken; he knows as much about me as I know about him. Which . . . isn't much.

Still. He and his family moved here after my dad had already been arrested. They have to know who I am.

Even if they do, though, they've never treated me or Gram any differently. Not the way the rest of this town has. When Gram had knee surgery two years ago, Darius brought us food, and I'm pretty sure he convinced some of the women from the AME church to drop off casseroles for us, too, even though we're white and don't go there. Jackson doesn't charge me when I order here sometimes, though I know Gram would be embarrassed if she knew how much it happened, so I try to pay more often than not.

But today when Jackson brings me a coffee I didn't order, he shakes his head when I try to pay him, so.

The diner doorbell rings and I glance up and there's Mavis, changed into a thick green sweater and even thicker glasses. She waves at me as she walks up to the counter. I watch as she orders something from Jackson and then takes a seat across from me.

"What'd you order?" I ask Mavis as she sits down. "The burgers are good."

She wrinkles her nose. I don't want to think it's as cute as I do. "I'm vegetarian. I just got oatmeal."

"You've got to be the first person who's ever ordered oatmeal from here. You couldn't get pancakes? Those are vegetarian."

"I didn't want pancakes, I wanted oatmeal," she says. "You gonna get anything besides coffee?"

I shake my head. "I—no." I don't want to tell her I can't really afford it. That I should eat whatever Gram's made at home. That even diner prices are too much for me, sometimes.

I really should stop spending my money on cigarettes. At least then I'd be able to have a burger.

"You know another way I can tell you aren't from around here?" I say, just to change the subject. "I think you're the only vegetarian in the county."

Mavis laughs. Well, snorts. It's cute.

"Is it for, like, personal reasons, or . . . ?" I trail off. Gram would smack me for asking this. Far too nosy.

"Health, but personal, too, yeah," she says. "Anyway. If you want fries or something, I can get them. My treat."

I squirm. "No, thanks."

"Come on. You're the only person who's actually talked to me today. Let me get you fries."

She waves down Darius and orders before I can stop her. I

give Darius a sheepish smile and he raises his eyebrows at me before looking back at Mavis, then back to me. Something flutters in my chest—hope, maybe.

For once I let it.

"Drove by the funeral on the way here," Mavis says. "You were right. I think the whole town is there. At least from the look of the parking lot."

I'm about to comment when our food arrives and I stop. The smell of her oatmeal makes my mouth water, cinnamon and other spices, and there's a giant pat of butter on top just melting into it.

I chew on a fry. Mavis takes one, too, then speaks again.

"Why *didn't* you go?" she asks. "Even if you didn't know her that well. Not like everyone in town knew her, and it seemed like they were all there."

The fry feels like a hard lump in my throat. I force myself to swallow.

"I think they're just there for the gossip," I say. "That sounds rude, but—"

"No," Mavis cuts me off. "You're right. That's what they're doing." Her shoulders tense. "Do you think they'll catch who did it?"

"I don't know," I say. Again, briefly, that hope bubbles up—she can't know about my dad. She wouldn't be asking me questions like this if she knew. "The sheriff's department is pretty small, but maybe they will."

“It’s fucked up,” Mavis says. “For her family. Their daughter dies and the whole town comes to stare and they don’t know who did it.”

“It is,” I agree, and some of the tension releases from her shoulders.

“God,” she says. “Do you think there are any suspects or anything? I mean—who kills teenage girls?”

Her question feels deliberate, and I press my shaking hands into my lap. She doesn’t know. I have to keep telling myself that. She seems too . . . direct. If she knew about my dad, she’d say so. She wouldn’t ask me a question like this.

Besides. I know who kills teenage girls. The who isn’t what she should be asking. It’s the *why*.

Is it because they’re young? Because they’re pretty? Because they’re full of potential and to some men that is so *infuriating*?

I never asked my dad why.

Well.

That’s a lie.

I asked him why *not*. The first time I visited him in prison. My hair was short but not shaved, not yet, and we’d sat across that glass from each other and I don’t know if it was because I’d started my period the week before and was upset and angry, or if I just wanted to piss him off, but I asked. The fact that I was younger than his victims wasn’t relevant, not to me. There were serial killers who’d killed their families, too.

“Why not me?”

He'd fixed me with a hard look. "What?"

"Why—why didn't you kill me?"

My throat had closed up. But I kept staring at him. Because I needed to know, and Gram wouldn't talk about it.

"Because," he finally said. "You're not a girl."

It's the only thing he ever got right about me.

"Sid?" Mavis's voice cuts through my thoughts, and I blink. I'm not at the prison. I'm back at the diner. I'm sitting across from a cute girl. I'm not sitting across from my dad.

And I'm older and I know why he didn't kill me. I know.

"Hey," I say, just to have something else to think about. "You . . . you mentioned something I should know about you? Or should've known, I guess? When we were behind the bleachers today."

Mavis's face falls. "Oh. Yeah. I, um, I'd rather not talk about it. If you don't already know, I don't want to be the one to tell you."

"I could look it up," I threaten. "I could just—I could Google it."

She nods. "Yeah. You could. But you won't."

"Why not?"

"Because you're too good for that, Sid," she says. "You're good at keeping secrets." She studies me again. "I could do the same to you, you know. Look you up. Find out why three people came up to me today and told me I should stay away from you."

"You could," I say. My pulse quickens. It feels like a leap, saying this. “But I don’t think you will, either.”

“No,” she says. “I won’t.”

Something in her face makes me believe her.

The bell above the door rings, and both Mavis and I turn. A steady stream of people from our school is starting to head in, all in black—mourners.

“A murder of crows,” I mutter, knowing it’s not funny, but Mavis looks at me and I catch a smile on her face before she goes back to her oatmeal.

When I get home, Gram’s smoking behind the screen door, her lips pursed, blowing smoke out through the screen. I don’t say anything, even though she hates when I do the same thing. She wasn’t thrilled when I started smoking at fifteen, filching cigarettes from her purse until she finally caught me and told me that if I was going to try to kill myself early, I had to buy my own packs.

“How was the funeral?” she asks.

“Dunno,” I say. “Didn’t go in.” I don’t add that no one wanted me there. She knows that well enough.

I kick off my shoes and go to stand by the door across from Gram. Before I moved in with her, Gram was the woman I saw twice a year at Christmas and Easter, when we got together with Dad’s family thirty minutes away in Kinston. She and Dad never talked much. I was the youngest of all the cousins by far, so I was always left out.

But when Dad was arrested, she was the one who took me in. Mom wasn't in the picture, had left when I was seven. She would write to me sometimes, but then when I turned ten, the card I tried to send her got returned, no forwarding address.

I didn't even know where she was until they tried to contact her when Dad was arrested. By then she'd moved all the way out to California. She had a new husband, a new family, a new life that didn't include a surly teenager whose father had just been arrested for murder.

Did she know? Did she know what Dad would become? Is that why she left? Or did she have no idea and leave for some other reason? It's something I've never been able to ask Dad, and Gram wouldn't know.

I looked her up online once, because I don't want to ask Gram about her, don't want to seem ungrateful. Found her Facebook profile and created my own fake account just so I could see her photos, scrolling through the ones she'd made public. Her and the new husband, both dressed in khaki and white, posing on a beach. Her holding a baby with the tiniest hands I'd ever seen, the caption under the photo reading "My fresh start."

I'd closed out the photo and cleared the browser before Gram could ever ask what I was doing. That was three years ago, and I haven't looked her up since. Better to just leave her to her fresh start.

I pull a cigarette out of the almost-empty carton in my jeans pocket and light it with Gram's lighter. She raises an eyebrow at me.

"Where'd you go instead of the funeral?"

"Went to the diner," I say, blowing smoke out. "Darius says hey."

"He didn't pay for you again, I hope."

"Naw," I say. "He didn't." Technically, this is true. Jackson paid for the coffee and Mavis paid for the fries.

I don't mention Mavis. Gram knows I like girls. But I've only known this girl for a day I don't want that bubble of possibility to burst yet. Don't want Gram to ask if Mavis knows about Dad. I want to live in that bubble where she doesn't know anything just a little bit longer.

Gram and I don't talk about Dad. She's never answered when I asked what she thought. If she was surprised at what he did. Or if she knew. If she ever doubted like I have. You read about these things, serial killers showing signs during childhood, torturing animals or setting fires or hitting their head on a swing.

I don't know the why. Why he did it. And if Gram does, she's not telling.

Like—who kills teenage girls?

Who kills a girl like June Hargrove?

"Who kills girls like us?"

The whisper is in my ear as clearly as if someone were standing next to me. I suppress a shudder.

I know whose voice it is.

I open the door the rest of the way and stomp out my half-smoked cigarette on the broken concrete step outside. Gram sighs but doesn't reprimand me, just takes a long drag off hers.

"I've got homework," I say, and she nods, and I retreat to my room, Lauren O'Malley's question echoing in my head.

Who kills girls like us?

I started hearing the girls after Dad was sentenced. The ghosts. I was fifteen, standing in the bathroom holding a pair of scissors, debating.

"Do it," a voice in my ear whispered, and I jumped. I couldn't see her but I knew who it was. Knew who *she* was. Lauren. The first girl my father killed.

The first ghost to talk to me.

I told the therapist about it, the one Gram made me go see. All of Dad's victims had made an appearance by then—Lauren, Alicia, Melissa, Dawn, Samantha. I told her about the girls, the ghosts, and she gave me a thin-lipped smile like she had expected this sort of capital-T Trauma.

"Do they ever tell you to do anything?"

"S-sometimes," I said, running my fingers through my short hair. She looked intrigued at that, her pen flying over her notebook.

"Like what?"

"Just—just cutting my hair."

"Do they ever tell you to hurt yourself, or other people?"

"No," I said. I swore she almost looked disappointed.

"Can you see them?"

"No," I said. I wasn't lying. I couldn't see them, never fully, just shadows at the corners of my vision. I didn't think that counted, not in the way she was asking.

"Do you hear them all the time, or only when you're upset?"

"When I'm upset," I answered, because I was already picking up on how the game was played. On what would happen if I answered her questions honestly.

She wrote me a prescription for Ativan that Gram only filled once, and the next time she asked about the ghosts, I said I didn't hear them anymore. That they went away when Dad was sentenced. She nodded.

"Trauma like yours can manifest itself in many different ways," she said. "I'm not surprised you thought you were hearing the girls. Do you think this is your way of trying to make sense of what your father did?"

"Yes," I said. "I think that's it."

She'd smiled that broad smile again and placed a cold hand over my own. "The girls aren't real, Sidney. Those girls are buried. They're at rest. You should leave them that way."

"Of course," I'd said, and I'd smiled, too.

That was the last session I had with Dr. Rainer. I'd gone home that day and told Gram I didn't want to do them anymore, and she'd sighed, but she hadn't argued. They were probably costing her more than we could afford, anyway.

And the girls *did* go away. Gradually at first, until one day when I was fifteen I realized I hadn't heard from them in months. They left me alone, and I thought it was over.

Until today.

But that doesn't mean anything. It can't, because they're not real. June's death was awful, a one-off, a fucking tragedy in a town that's too full of tragedies, but it doesn't mean there's another serial killer here.

I boot up the ancient desktop in my room, wait impatiently for the log-in screen to load. I'd almost be better off using the library computers than this one. Gram only keeps it around so I can do homework, and because she likes to play solitaire when I'm at school.

Five minutes later when my browser loads, I type in June Hargrove's name, looking for any scrap of information I can find, an autopsy report, internet theories. Mavis's comment comes back to me and I shrug it off, knowing I'm paying more attention to June now that she's dead than I ever did when she was alive.

I'm no better than the rest of this town.

But as I scroll through the search results, it quickly becomes clear that news of her death has barely made it outside of North Carolina. There's no mention of how she died. No mention of if her head was shaved.

I could ask Sally Louise, if she'd even talk to me. But I shouldn't. I don't need to get involved in this. I don't need to prove my dad had nothing to do with it. He couldn't. He's in prison.

But—

LAUREN O'MALLEY
ALICIA GRAVES
MELISSA WAGNER
DAWN SCHAEFER
SAMANTHA MARKHAM

Their voices chorus in my head, and I clamp my hands over my ears, but it doesn't do any good because I can still hear them—

Of course he could have done it.

Look what he did to us.

Lauren O'Malley: January 8, 2008

LAUREN O'MALLEY was the first girl my father killed. There were only a few posters for her, because she was one missing girl in a small town, and she wasn't the right kind of girl, with her short hair and too-loud laugh.

I like to think that Lauren and I would have been friends if we'd been the same age.

Would have, if my father hadn't killed her.

This is what they will say about Lauren O'Malley, after, in grocery store lines, at church, at school:

She was bright. She was young. Her life ended too soon. What a nice girl. What a tragedy.

This is what they will say at home behind closed doors, whispered among family members, classmates:

Who accepts a ride from a stranger in this day and age?

She should've known better.

Well, you know how her mother is. No one's been around to teach her those things.

Girl gets in a car with a stranger, she deserves what's coming to her.

A girl's car gets a flat two miles from her house, and she swears, even though her mother says it's impolite.

She knows she should've gotten that tire replaced when she went to get her oil changed last week, but she could barely afford the oil change—hell, they can barely afford the car—and she thought she'd have more time before the tire wore through.

She always thought she'd have more time.

She was late getting home Saturday and she knows her mother will kill her if she's home late again today, mostly because her mother found out yesterday that Lauren was out late because of Jessica Reed, and everyone knows what kind of girl Jessica Reed is.

Lauren doesn't plan on telling her she was out late kissing Jessica Reed. Doesn't plan on telling her mom they've already decided to meet up again this weekend and go to the movies.

Lauren flips her phone open and tries to call her mom, tell her she'll be late and the car got a flat and can she come get her, but the landline rings and rings and no one picks up.

Lauren sighs and starts walking.

Half a mile in, it begins to rain. Lauren forgot to wear a rain jacket (yet another thing her mother will kill her for), so she stands at the side of the road and sticks her thumb out.

She knows the warnings. She's heard the stories.

But all the stories she's heard are from, like, the seventies and involve girls on big highways, not small North Carolina back roads.

She'll be fine. She's only two miles away from home and it's raining, and she knows everyone in this town.

When a car slows and flashes its brights at her, she doesn't think twice about getting in.

Her mother looks at the clock.

It's midnight. Lauren still isn't home.

She calls her cell phone and it goes to voice mail, and she swears if she finds out that girl was with Jessica Reed again, she'll definitely kill her this time.

Chapter Four

SAVANNAH BAUNACH'S seat is empty in homeroom the next day. After the first bell rings we all sit there, staring at it as if we can will her to show up.

But she doesn't. Five more minutes pass by and finally Mrs. Eddins calls roll, like she's been waiting for Savannah to show up, too. Her eyes stay on Savannah's and June's empty seats as she calls out our names, and only Mavis's arrival a minute later finally snaps her attention somewhere else.

Savannah's fine, I try to convince myself. She's probably just out sick. It is winter. I can hear two people sniffling behind me who probably *should* have stayed home.

But I can't help but think this is how the murders started last time, and I know I'm not the only one. None of us were old enough back then to really absorb the details of what was going on, but I remember the girls. Their faces on the news; girls I'd seen around town cheering at football games, smoking in the parking lot of the Piggly Wiggly.

I remember Dad would always change the channel if he came in and the news was talking about the disappearances, saying I was too young to be seeing such frightening things like that. That it was nothing I needed to worry about.

Worry hadn't crossed my mind before he said that. Lauren was the only one who'd been reported missing at the time, and everyone thought she'd just run off..

Savannah's fine. She has to be. She'll show up by lunch, saying she's overslept, hanging off of Craig Hutchens's arm. Just because June was murdered doesn't mean anything has happened to Savannah.

"Or she's not fine," a voice says in my head. *"Or she's been drowned in the lake, just like us."*

This time I can't tell if it's a ghost or just my own fear. Dr. Rainer called this "catastrophizing" when I was a kid. Taking something that had happened and spinning it in my head to be far worse than it actually was.

But how could I not? Sheriff Kepler had asked if my dad was home, and the next thing I knew Dad was being arrested. How could I not think of the worst-case scenario for anything that happened after that? I had to think about it so I could be prepared.

So I'd know what to do if it happened again.

The bell rings for first period and we all gather our stuff to leave, though most of us give a wide berth to Savannah's empty desk, like we're all trying to avoid it. Like if we acknowledge she's gone it'll be bad luck.

The same thing happens in English. Even Mavis shoots a glance at Savannah's empty desk before she sits down in what was June's seat. Mrs. Hill, at least, asks if anyone's heard from Savannah. We all shake our heads no.

"All right then. Partner up to discuss chapter nine," she says, and I sigh, get ready to work alone again.

But then Mavis twists around in her seat. "Partners?" she asks, and I let myself grin, trying my hardest to ignore Kate Langley, Savannah's best friend, as she goes to partner with Mrs. Hill instead.

I sit under the bleachers again at lunch, and to my surprise, Mavis joins me. Maybe I shouldn't be surprised, since she partnered with me in English, but there's a difference between having to talk about a book together in class and eating lunch together.

"Mind if I?" she asks, but sits down before I can reply. I go ahead and stub out my cigarette, never mind that I'd only started it and shouldn't waste them. A couple other seniors walk by, and Mavis glances at them. My stomach knots, but they don't even look twice at us, and I can breathe easy again.

"So what other classes are you taking?" I ask, because it's the only thing I can think to ask her and the only classes I've seen her in are English and calculus.

"Um. Psychology, yearbook, and they're letting me do AP Art since I came from an arts high school and was pretty advanced, I guess?" Her voice goes soft and she ducks her head.

"So what do you . . . make art of?" I ask, and she laughs.

"I paint. Mainly. Occasionally I'll sculpt or do charcoal, but I mostly paint. Sometimes people. Sometimes abstract things." She shrugs. "I haven't done much since we moved. But Mr. Waters wants a portfolio of three different mediums, including painting, so I guess I'll have to pick it back up. I haven't felt like unpacking my paints just yet."

Something about the way she says it, plus what she said yesterday, makes me decide not to push it.

"Anyway," she says. "Um. Can I ask you something?"

"Go ahead."

"How do you—how do you want me to refer to you? If I'm talking about you, I mean."

"You're talking about me?" I ask. My face flushes.

"No, I mean—if I do. If I ever do. Like, in class if you're not there and I'm like, 'Hey, can I take Sid *blank* assignments,' what pronoun should I use?"

I can't help it. I start laughing.

"What's so funny?"

"You're asking about my pronouns," I say.

"How is that funny?"

"Because—because you're the first person who's ever done that for me," I say, and suddenly she's right, suddenly it doesn't seem so funny anymore. "Am I the only person you've asked?"

"No," she says. "I asked someone yesterday in art class."

"Oh," I say. I don't know how to respond. If she'd only asked me because she thought my answer would be important, that would be one thing. But then again, no one's *ever* asked me. I don't know how to feel about this at all. I haven't given it much thought. Sometimes I'll have fleeting ideas of being out of here, being in a big city where no one knows me, introducing myself and saying, "Yeah, you can use 'they' to refer to me," as if it's the most natural thing in the world.

But here? Where everyone already has an idea of who they think I am?

"I—I'd use they, I think," I say. "But you won't hear anyone use that for me here. And I don't know if I want you to use that at school or anything."

"Fair," Mavis says, but now that I've started trying to explain this to her I can't stop myself, the words all coming out in a rush. "It's not—like. It's not really important to me here, it just—I know down here people are going to see me as a boy or a girl and trying to explain that I don't see myself as either is just—" I pause, frustrated that I don't have the words, that I don't know how to explain what I am, how I feel. "I mean . . . yeah. My gram knows but we don't talk about it, too confusing for her and I don't think it matters that much to her, anyway—not in a bad way, just in a it doesn't make a difference to her one way or another . . . way, so . . ." I'm rambling. I'm overthinking. "Yeah," I finish. "Um. What—I guess, what pronouns do you use?"

"She/her," Mavis says. "Can you answer one more thing for me?"

"Sure."

"Your . . . Graham?"

I laugh. "Grandmother. Grandma? No, she hates that. Yeah. My gram."

"Like the cracker?"

"Just G-R-A-M."

"Oh," Mavis says. "I . . . okay."

"What do you call your grandparents?"

"Um. I've only got the one, so Nan."

I scoff. "That sounds so proper."

"Better than a cracker," Mavis says, and I laugh. She leans back on her hands and tips her head back, closing her eyes. I watch as she does so, trying not to stare yet knowing I'm staring, anyway.

God, I like this girl.

Savannah doesn't show up by fourth period, either. When the bell rings, her boyfriend, Craig Hutchens, is the last one out of the classroom, like he was hoping she'd show up before the day ended and doesn't want to let go of that possibility yet.

Out in the parking lot I spot Jenny, Savannah's younger sister. She's looking around like she's lost, and I realize Savannah must normally drive her to and from school. I wonder who's picking her up today. Which of her parents decided to come.

Gram wouldn't come get me even if I asked. I can't blame her for that, for not wanting to deal with the stares and gossip. When Dad was arrested, she was mentioned far more often than I was.

She tried to hide it from me—all of it. Wouldn't even let me visit Dad in prison until I was fifteen.

I figured it out from the news only a few weeks after the arrest. Maybe that's awful. I hadn't meant to find out that way; Gram had been out and the TV had been left on and then there was my dad's face, and there were the faces of the girls he'd killed; girls whose missing posters I'd seen all around town as a child. The grisly, awful facts of how he'd strangled them, shaved their heads, and dumped their bodies in Cardinal Lake. Facts I wasn't supposed to know at that age.

I turned the TV off before Gram came home. Spent that afternoon looking up as many details as I could, knowing that once she came back I wouldn't be allowed to again. I never told her that was how I'd found out.

A few months later, I went to live with Gram permanently. She thought I might want some stability, so we stayed in Cardinal Creek. Dad was still awaiting trial. She sold her house in Kinston and bought the trailer, sent in all the forms so her new address wouldn't be on the voter registry and no one would be able to contact us. At least on that front she was successful, though I know if someone really wanted to find us, they could. Some podcasters a couple years ago got Gram's landline off Reddit supposedly, called up with cheerful northern accents asking if we wanted to talk. If I wanted to talk.

I didn't. And the only time Gram and I did was the day Dad was sentenced. I hadn't started hearing the girls yet, not then. I knew what Dad had done, was just beginning to grapple with the fact that he was guilty. Even that day when it was made official, I still wanted to hold out some hope, I still didn't want to fully believe it.

"Gram?"

She'd come to tuck me into bed, had been doing so since I'd started staying with her, even though I was too old for that. I was sitting up, my chin tucked on my bony knees, my teeth clacking as I spoke. "Do you really think he did it?"

She hadn't answered. She'd sighed and pursed her lips, more a confirmation than words would have been. No denial, no "Now why would you ask a thing like that?" Just silence and a nod, and then she left me alone to deal with that information and she has ever since.

Savannah Baunach isn't in class Thursday, either.

By Friday the posters have gone back up.

Have You Seen This Girl?

I think it's happening again.

One missing girl is a family's problem.

Two missing girls?

It becomes the town's problem.

On Friday, the third official day Savannah is missing, there's an assembly at school and an announcement that there will be a search party tomorrow and we can help if we want.

After lunch we all crowd into the gym for the assembly; it still smells like body spray and sweat from last period. I sit on the top row of bleachers, all the way in the back. Since Savannah went missing, the whispers and rumors have doubled. I can guess at least half of them are about me.

I put my earbuds in. I won't learn anything useful at this assembly. No one's going to confirm if Savannah's disappearance is related to my dad, or if it's related to June's disappearance, or how June died. It's going to be a lot of empty promises and tears and details about the search party tomorrow.

Mavis walks in with the rest of her art class, Lilah not far behind her. Mavis looks my way and waves, and I watch Lilah follow her gaze, her mouth twisting into a frown. Lilah hated me even before she found out what my father did, because I was Sally Louise's best friend and that was all she ever wanted—that and the popularity that came with it.

But then Sally Louise's dad arrested mine, and she stopped talking to me, and a week later Lilah was hanging off her arm like she was supposed to be there all along.

It used to bother me. It doesn't anymore.

Lilah splits off to go sit with Sally Louise and the other cheerleaders, even though she didn't make the squad this year—something about her grades, which I'm sure her mother was thrilled about. I half expect Mavis to go join her. But instead, Mavis starts up the stairs toward the back row. Toward me.

"Hey," she says, swinging her backpack over her shoulder and taking a seat next to me. "What're you doing all the way up here?"

"Not a fan of assemblies," I say, taking my earbuds out. "Why didn't you go sit with Lilah, or your class?"

"Because I wanted to sit with you," she says, blushing.

"Oh," I say. I press my hands to my knees, wish for a cigarette. She doesn't say anything else after that. She doesn't ask if I think they'll find Savannah, doesn't toss out theories like the rest of my classmates have today—theories like Savannah was so upset about June that she killed herself and this is just to cover it up, which I don't believe. She doesn't act fake-concerned for a girl she barely knows. She sits in silence with me until Principal Johnston takes the stage, and then she leans forward intently.

I zone out, even though I don't put my earbuds back in. I don't need to pay attention to what he has to say. Whatever it is isn't going to make a difference. Not to June. Not to Savannah.

"I think you *should* pay attention, though."

I freeze. But it's not Mavis asking. It's not Sally Louise come to chastise me. It's not even Lauren O'Malley.

The smell of rot hits my nose and I turn, and there, sitting next to me, is June Hargrove. Her skin has a bluish cast, her lips almost purple. There is so much dirt under her fingernails. She's dressed identically to me, almost mocking, in an outfit she never would have worn when she was alive, a hoodie pulled over her head.

A scream crawls up my throat, but I stifle it down. June cocks her head and smiles at me. She hasn't started to visibly decay. Not yet. But the stink of rot makes me gag.

You're not real, I think. *You're not real.*

"I'm real," she says, and smiles, the inside of her mouth black.

I need to get out of here.

"You need to pay attention," she says again. She leans over, her breath cold in my face. Under the rot is the smell of the lake. "Or it's going to be too late for poor Savannah." She cocks her head, like she's listening to something far away. "It sounds like you don't have much time left."

Before I can ask what she means, she's gone, and I'm left covering my nose and trying not to gag. A few people glance my way, but as soon as I meet their eyes they whip their heads around back to the front. It takes several minutes for my heart to calm back down.

I saw June. I *saw* her and no one else did, but she was right there; she was sitting next to me, so close she could almost touch me and—

How could I have seen her? She's dead. She's dead and I've only ever heard the ghosts, not seen them. They're not real. They're just in my head. I haven't heard them since I was fifteen.

Except for the other day. And now June, except she wasn't just a voice, she was real. I could feel her cold breath. I could smell the rot from the lake. Lauren, Alicia, Melissa, Dawn, Samantha, they've only just ever been voices in my head, shadows at the corners of my vision. Not real girls filling my nose with the scent of decay.

June Hargrove is dead, I think. She's a corpse in the ground, she's a girl who died, and my father isn't responsible. Just like he's not responsible for Savannah.

This has nothing to do with him.

But I won't be sure until I know how June died. And there's only one person I can ask about that.

June Hargrove: January 8, 2018

MR. WOLF is being difficult to her on purpose. First by ignoring her email about her grade from last semester—which, to be fair, she only noticed the day before classes ended—to never setting a direct time to meet with her about it. Which is how she's ended up waiting outside his door until 3:45, hoping that he'll actually talk to her about changing it.

Savannah's the one who insisted she make a fuss about her grade. She was originally just going to accept it, but Savannah pushed her to talk to Mr. Wolf, so now here she is. Especially since she realized that it would bring her up to an eighty instead of the seventy-nine she currently has. She wouldn't be so insistent on it except for the fact that she's only one point away from a B, and her GPA needs all the help it can get.

Besides. She did the extra work, after all. She should get credit for it.

He finally lets her in, and the meeting takes all of ten minutes, during which she makes a case for all the extra assignments and credit she did last semester, and tells him that if the grade isn't updated by next week, she'll be back again to ask about it.

By the time she finally walks out to her car, it's almost four. She's one of the only people in the parking lot—it's too early in the semester for anyone else to be staying behind.

But June Hargrove does not make it to her car. She takes too long to dig her keys out of her purse, and then someone's arms wrap around her waist, and for a second she thinks it's one of her friends, Craig or Savannah, even though she told them not to wait for her, that she'd see them later.

But the voice in her ear is too deep and she can't catch what it says before there's a cloth over her mouth and she's breathing in big gasping panicked breaths that only make it worse, and she can feel her body slipping, her mind slipping, and the last thing she thinks of, the last thing that crosses her mind, is she wishes she'd stayed ten minutes longer to make sure Mr. Wolf actually changed her grade, instead of just accepting his word for it and leaving.

Chapter Five

THE NEXT day is the search party for Savannah, and it feels like practically the whole town has congregated in the town center. Sheriff Kepler called a meeting there to organize the search parties; Savannah's parents will say a few words and then we're splitting up. Half of the groups are going to search the woods near Savannah's house, the last place she was seen, and then the sheriff and his men will lead a few different groups around the lake.

We can choose which group we go with. I'm going to whichever one Sally Louise is in, as long as I can avoid her dad while doing so. I need to talk to her. I need to find out the details of what happened to June.

What might have already happened to Savannah.

The rumors that their disappearances are linked have me on edge. Of course I know why everyone's thinking that. It's the same reason causing a sick feeling to bubble up in my stomach every time I think about it—that this has something to do with my dad.

I hang at the back of the crowd to avoid everyone, even though that feels almost impossible here. Most everyone from my high school has shown up, and their parents keep shooting me dirty looks, even though I have classes with their kids and see them every day. Savannah's own parents and her sister, Jenny, stand at the front, across from the sheriff. Jenny's leaning on her mom. Next to her is Craig. He looks somehow worse than Savannah's parents do, his face haggard.

I like Craig. He sits behind me in civics, and while he's never talked to me, I don't get the feeling he hates me, the way I do from some of my classmates.

It looks like everyone's here with their families, or at least most of them are.

No one came with me. I asked Gram if she wanted to come, but she just complained about her back and said she wasn't traipsing around the woods for something she wasn't even sure we'd find.

I dropped it after that. Who knows if her back's actually hurting or if she just doesn't want to endure the same hostile stares I'm getting.

Dad helped. When the search was for his victims. I remember because he left me with a babysitter for one of them, one of the only times after Mom had left. Aunt Paula was unavailable, or maybe he just didn't want to see her—we saw my aunts as often as we saw Gram, despite the fact they only lived a town over. I don't know why he didn't ask Gram.

I don't remember what he said that night. I wish I could. Or maybe I don't. I just remember him coming back late, because I was already in bed. I remember he hadn't taken his boots off, that they were muddy, and when he came to tuck me in I remember laughing about it, saying they were gross.

The media loved that, I found out later. That he helped look for his victims and then came back to tuck me into bed. It was in all the articles. It's not uncommon for serial killers to help with the search for their victims. Some think it takes suspicion off of them. Others get off on it, seeing other people's reactions.

Whoever took Savannah, is he here? Is he helping like my dad did?

I scan the faces in the crowd. I know most of them, but that doesn't matter. The ones that do make eye contact with me look away quickly, or else their mouths twist in disgust. Lilah Crenshaw and her parents stand near the sheriff and Sally Louise, and when I meet their eyes, the three of them glare at me with identical expressions of hatred. Only Sheriff Kepler's and Sally Louise's expressions don't change.

I shouldn't be here. If I help, it won't matter. Dad helped, and he was a killer. If I don't help, they'll say I don't care. I'm damned either way but at least if I went home I wouldn't have to endure the staring.

"You need to help," Alicia Graves whispers in my ear, and I stiffen. My head whips around, but there's no one there. Not even June.

At least I can't see Alicia.

If I can't see her, then the therapist was right, and the girls' voices are just a projection of my own feelings about what Dad did.

But June wasn't a projection. June was real. I could smell her rotting. I could *see* her.

What am I supposed to do if she shows up today? If Savannah shows up today? Will that mean she's actually dead?

Catastrophizing. I'm catastrophizing. I'm about to really leave, voices and ghosts be damned, when Savannah's dad steps up to the podium and asks for a prayer to find his daughter, and everyone bows their heads.

I can't leave now. They'll hear me. So I bow my head but keep my eyes open. Someone brushes by me and I think it's June. I look up sharply, but it's Mavis. Her cheeks are flushed and she's breathing hard.

Someone's told her, I think. Someone here, they had to have.

But the grin she shoots me tells me she doesn't know, and that, at least, makes me breathe a little easier. I don't know what to do with her, what to think. I've never had a chance like this before.

Her hand is so close to mine. I could reach over and take it.

But then the moment of silence is over, and everyone's back to looking around, looking at *me*, and I can't.

◆ ◆ ◆

Sheriff Kepler thanks everyone for coming to help, and his boys pass out maps that have been split into grids marking the places where everyone will search. I'm impressed they're so organized, but then again, Sheriff Kepler is in charge. We didn't even have a search and rescue department until he became sheriff five years ago. It takes a while for people to group up. I hang back, telling Mavis we'll just go with whichever group the sheriff is leading.

If she's wondering why I'm not pushing myself into the crowd with everyone else, she doesn't ask. I excuse myself for a cigarette while she volunteers to grab a map, taking long enough that by the time I'm done most of the other people have started driving off, some to the subdivision five minutes from here where the Baunachs live, and others to the closest access point to the lake.

"Let's go to the lake," I say, and start off that way. Mavis jogs to catch up with me.

"Everyone else is driving," she says. "Isn't it far?"

"I can bike," I say. "It's not that bad."

"Or you can let me drive us," she says. "Please? I'll get lost without you."

My face flushes at that, this implication that she needs me even when she's got a perfectly good maps app on her phone, but I don't argue. We drive to the lake, and I'm relieved when we pull up and Sally Louise is getting out of the car with her dad. The feeling dissipates when I see Lilah get out of the car next to hers, but at least her parents aren't with her. Maybe they didn't actually want to help beyond showing up.

Mavis doesn't say much until we reach the edge of the woods. If we continue through them for a mile and a half or so, we'll reach the lake where June Hargrove was found. The lake my dad used for his victims.

It's no wonder it took them so long to be found. The lake is huge: almost nineteen miles across. It's a wonder we aren't searching it, but it's probably easier for Sheriff Kepler to organize all of us through the woods than the lake—besides, they'd probably need some specialized equipment to search the entire lake, something I'm sure they don't have.

"What do you think we're looking for?" I ask her, just to have something to say and because I really don't know other than we're looking for Savannah.

For her body, I think, but I don't dare say that out loud.

"Any sign of her, probably," Mavis says. "Clothes or fibers or things she could've left behind; shoe prints . . ."

"Jesus," I say. "I didn't think you'd actually have an answer for that."

"My mom's into true crime," Mavis says, but she bites her lip and doesn't elaborate. An anxious look crosses her face, one that mirrors the anxiety in my own stomach. If her mom is into true crime—

Would she know who I am?

I almost ask Mavis why her parents aren't also out here searching, but then stop myself. If I ask where hers are, she'll ask where Gram is. I don't feel like lying to her today, at least not directly.

"Savannah!" someone calls, and both Mavis and I turn. It's Lilah, her hands cupped around her mouth. Beside her is Sally Louise, and behind them a few more people from our school.

If they see Mavis with me, what will they say? Sally Louise wouldn't be that cruel, but that doesn't mean the others wouldn't.

My heart skips a beat when I catch a flash of brown hair, then, thinking it's June. But it's not. Just some other girl in my class. It takes me a second to regain my breath, and even longer than that to realize Mavis has stopped walking.

"Actually," she says. "Um. Being out here is—it's a lot. And I don't know this area so I don't know how much help I'll be, so would you mind if I go . . . if I go see if they need supplies or something? I'll meet you once it's over. I'm sorry," she adds, and before I can even reply she's gone, disappeared back the way we came.

"Oh," I say softly to the empty space where she was. I debate chasing after her for a second, just to see if she's all right, but then Lilah's laughter reaches my ears, and I don't. I can't afford to be seen leaving here after only five minutes.

She knows about Dad, I think, then shake it off. It's not a ghost whispering that to me, it's just my own fear. I keep my head down and go back to searching, if only to keep the ghosts and my own anxiety at bay. I stay a good distance away from Lilah and Sally Louise, though I can still occasionally hear their voices calling for Savannah. Their voices never really grow fainter, which tells me they aren't as far from me as I'd like.

We're not going to find anything, not today. I give up on looking for Savannah and instead begin to follow Sally and Lilah, hoping they don't notice me. I still need to talk to Sally.

After another half hour, someone blows a whistle to call off the search, even though there's still plenty of daylight left. We've made it almost a mile through the woods, and I spot Lilah's jacket as she and Sally start to head back.

Now or never.

"Sally!" I call, and she stops walking. Lilah does, too, and I jog over to them. Lilah's face twists in disgust when I get closer.

"I thought for sure you would've bailed by now," she says. "Didn't think you'd stay out here this long."

I bite my tongue to resist pointing out the fact that Lilah's own parents didn't even come to the actual search, but I don't. "I want to help," I say instead, looking at Sally—not Lilah.

"I'm sure the Baunachs are *thrilled* you're here helping," Lilah scoffs. "What do you *really* want?"

"I need to talk to you," I say, again just looking at Sally. "Please. It's important."

She must see the desperation on my face because she sighs, but she doesn't start walking away. Lilah folds her arms across her chest, but she doesn't leave, either.

When it's clear I'm not going to talk while Lilah's still there, Sally Louise sighs. "Lilah, can you go tell Dad I'll be a minute?" she asks, and Lilah looks shocked before glaring at her, only walking away when Sally Louise sighs again.

Sally turns back to me. Strands of her blond hair are escaping her ponytail, but it still looks artistic, like she styled it that way.

"What's so important, Sid?" she asks. I pause. Her tone isn't full of malice, just exhaustion.

"I . . ." I swallow. "I need to know how June Hargrove died."

Sally crosses her arms in front of her chest. "Why do you think I'd know that?"

"Because your dad's the sheriff."

"Dad doesn't tell me everything."

"Come on," I say. I almost reach out for her, but I don't. "Please, Sally, I need to know."

She doesn't ask me why. She already knows. Her dad arrested mine, after all. She probably understands my motivation more than anyone else in this town.

"I can't tell you that, Sid," she says, but she's biting her lip, the same way she did when we were twelve and she would lie to her dad about something. I watched her do it once, say she had no idea where her lunch had gone, that someone must have taken it out of her lunch box, when I knew she'd given it to me earlier that day.

"Can you just answer one question for me?" I ask. "Please."

"Sid, I—" She shakes her head. "Fine. One question."

"Was . . ." My mouth is dry. "Was her head shaved?"

Sally Louise looks at me for a long moment.

"Yes," she says. "It was."

I stumble out of the woods in a daze.

June's head was shaved. June's head was shaved, which means someone is copying my father. That June's murder, Savannah's disappearance, aren't random.

Someone is copying my father.

I don't know what to do with this knowledge. I wanted Sally Louise to confirm it, but now that I know that it's happening—

The sinking in my stomach gets worse, because if someone's copying my father, then Savannah Baunach is most likely already dead.

"Good job, Nancy Drew."

June.

I almost collide with her, and I freeze, my muscles tensing, my fingers scraping against the bark of a nearby tree as I try to keep myself upright. She's not wearing a hoodie, not this time. She's in something closer to what she would have worn alive: a tight pink shirt and jeans.

Her head is shaved.

"You're not real," I choke out before glancing around to make sure no one's watching me. They aren't, for once; there are a handful of people traipsing through the woods now, and I don't see Mavis yet.

June's icy fingers land on my arm, dripping with lake water. I flinch, but she holds me tight. When she finally removes her hand, there's a wet handprint on my hoodie.

"I'm not real?" she says, and laughs. "Try again."

"If you're real, then—then *help* me," I beg. My mouth is cotton dry.

"Why would I do that?" she asks. "It's so much more fun if you piece it together on your own."

"But we . . . Savannah—"

"Savannah's dead," June says flatly.

"If she's dead, then why don't I see her?"

"Maybe she doesn't want to visit you," June says. "You're really good at making our deaths about you, aren't you?" She pushes my shoulder, lightly; I step back to keep from falling. Before I can retort, say anything else, she vanishes, leaving behind the feeling of lake water in my bones.

Mavis finds me standing at the edge of the woods a minute later, clutching at my damp sleeve. "Hey," she says. "Looks like it's over. Sorry for—are you okay?"

"Fine," I say. "Where'd you go?"

"Oh I just waited by the car until I saw people leaving." She shrugs. "So do you . . . do you wanna do something?"

"Like what?"

"Well, I'm starving," she says. "We could get dinner."

My stomach growls just as she says it, and she laughs. "See? Your stomach agrees with me. Let's go eat. Is there anywhere around here that's not fast food or the diner?"

The lightness of her tone is jarring after what just happened with June, but I seize on the chance at normalcy. "There's a pizza place like a mile up the road," I say.

"Wanna do that?"

"Yeah," I say.

"Cool. You can drive my car if you want, I don't mind."

"I—I don't know how to drive," I say. "And I can just bike there, anyway—"

"It's too far for you to bike," she says, and I'm about to say that I normally ride much farther than a mile when she looks at me pleadingly. "Come on. Please? Just put it in my trunk and I'll drive."

I'm about to protest again, because I don't want to owe her, but then I spot Lilah Crenshaw and think about having to go and get my bike alone where anyone from this town can see me, and I give in.

Ten minutes later we're at Sal's Pizza, the only non-chain place besides the diner in a fifteen-mile radius. The lot is almost empty, and I'm relieved because that means that we'll be way less likely to run into anyone I know, and after the looks I got today, I don't want them to see me with Mavis.

She's cute when she drives, drumming her fingers on the

steering wheel, changing the radio every fifteen seconds because it's nothing but commercials.

I'm grateful the car ride is short, because it means I don't have to spend long worrying if June is going to show up in the back seat.

We take our seats inside the almost-empty pizza place. Mavis grabs a laminated menu and passes it to me. I wrinkle my nose at the grease on it, but at least it means the pizza will probably be good. It's either good here or really mediocre, depending on the day.

"How's the pizza here?" Mavis says. "Maybe I should've asked that before we came."

"Well, it's the best pizza in town," I say, deadpan. She looks at me. "It's the only pizza in town," I add, and she shakes her head.

"I'm sure it's fine," she says. "It's not Chicago style so I'm not gonna be able to compare it, so that's good, at least."

"I don't like Chicago style. Too much bread."

"No such thing," Mavis says. "I'm just gonna get a couple slices."

"You may want to rethink the couple slices—they're huge," I say, and she rolls her eyes.

"I'm sure I can handle it."

"Don't say I didn't warn you," I say, and she laughs.

I look down at my own menu. If she's getting two slices, I can, too, since they don't cost much. Hell, since she's driving,

I can take some home to Gram.

We talk about the weather while we're waiting, how I think it's cold but Mavis is in a light jacket, saying it's nothing compared to Chicago. I wouldn't know; I've never been outside the state, have hardly been outside of town except to go to Raleigh to see my dad.

I'd like to go to California someday. Beaches and smog and a crowd I could get lost in where no one knows who I am. Eternal sunshine.

There's a California postcard on my wall from my mom. It's stereotypical: some place called Moonstone Beach, seagulls and a sunset and a *Wish you were here!* in blue cursive font.

I don't even remember what she wrote on the back of it. The picture's the only reason I kept it.

"Hey," Mavis says. "I'm sorry about bailing during the search. I thought . . . I dunno." She gives me a tight smile.

"Oh," I say. "I mean. It's fine. That's—yeah, it's gotta be hard, right? I mean. Searching for a girl our age. It sucks."

There's part of me that wants to ask her why she really bailed, but I push it away. I don't think she'd answer me, and I don't want to ruin this moment by thinking about what we spent the afternoon doing.

"It does," Mavis agrees. She looks like for a minute she wants to say more, but then the waitress brings out our orders, and she dives in without saying anything else. I watch her take a bite of her pizza—bell pepper, olives, and extra cheese.

"That's gross," I say. "Who puts black olives on pizza?"

"Lots of people," she counters. She takes a sip of her drink and looks at me. "Didn't you order a drink?"

"I did, but—" It's no big deal, I start to say, but she's already flagging down the waitress.

"My friend didn't get their drink," she says, and the waitress looks at me apologetically before hurrying off.

Their. It's so small but it isn't, this one word no one has ever used for me before. Mavis glances at me worriedly as soon as our waitress leaves.

"Was that okay? It just came out. I'm sorry—"

I reach for her hand before I can really stop myself. "It's fine," I say. "I . . . thank you. Don't use it at school, though, since I'm still getting used to it, but—thank you."

Mavis beams, and that smile lights me up from the inside.

Maybe I should tell her. For god's sake, she got my pronouns right. Who would do that down here? Maybe she would be understanding about my dad. Maybe I could be the one to tell her and the two of us could still have a chance.

"Mavis, I . . ."

But whatever else I was going to say is interrupted by the waitress bringing my drink, and I pull my hand away from Mavis's. Things like that might be safe in Durham, or Chapel Hill, but out here in the sticks it's always a gamble.

"Thanks," I mutter to the waitress, and she heads back to the counter and leans on it, taking out her cell phone. She can't be more than a few years older than me. She probably went to my high school, though if she did I don't recognize her.

She narrowly escaped being a victim, just by virtue of that. Too young for my dad, too old for whoever's killing girls now.

For whoever's copying my dad now.

I take another bite of my pizza, determined to enjoy it, to enjoy this moment with Mavis without thinking about the girls.

Without thinking about the fact that June's head was shaved.

"So," Mavis says as she picks up her second slice. "Do you really not know how to drive?"

"Nope," I say. "I'm surprised you do. Thought people in big cities didn't need cars."

Mavis laughs at this. "We lived outside Chicago, so the car was necessary, and Dad wanted to make sure I knew how before we moved down here. What about you?"

"Are you asking why I *don't* know how to drive?"

"Yeah," she says. "I guess I am."

"Because we only have one car and I was too busy last spring to take drivers' ed." I don't add that the drivers' ed course was taught by one of Sheriff Kepler's deputies. Sergeant Dunn. I don't add that he was one of the men who helped arrest my dad. "Plus, it's expensive." Even though it was only sixty-five dollars through the school, that's sixty-five dollars Gram and I spent on better things than me driving. "And I have a bike."

"I can't believe you really bike everywhere."

"I don't go many places," I say, knowing it sounds pathetic even as I say it. Mavis looks at me.

"You should learn then," she says.

"How to go places?"

"How to drive! I could teach you. My dad taught me how." She grins. "Come on, it'll be perfect. Plus, we can spend more time together."

"You want to spend more time with me?" I ask, partly because I really want to hear how she'll answer this and partly for the blush that crawls up her face when I do.

"Maybe I do," she says. "Please? Your gram won't mind, will she?"

"As long as we're not practicing in her car," I say. "She'll probably be thrilled." If I can drive, I can run errands for her, and she can stop getting Johnny Pritchard to do it.

"Cool," Mavis says, and she eyes the crusts of my pizza. "So . . . are you going to finish those?"

"You can have them," I say, pushing the plate toward her. As far as I'm concerned, she can have whatever she wants, because she's the first person in five years to ever tell me she wants to spend time with *me.*

I can't sleep.

Mavis dropped me off two hours ago, and all I'm thinking about is the way she looked when she suggested the driving lessons, the way she said, "We can spend more time together."

But I still biked the last half mile up the road so Mavis wouldn't see our house, not ready to expose her to that part of my life just yet, this girl with her clean car that probably cost more than our whole trailer did.

Gram gave me a once-over when I came in, like she knew I was out with someone, but she didn't say anything. I didn't tell her how the search went; didn't want June to show up again.

We don't talk about what Dad did. And now that I know this is related, that someone is copying Dad—

How am I supposed to talk about it to her at all? About the girls I hear, about June Hargrove's ghost showing up when I don't want her to?

About my fear Savannah might do the same thing?

I can't.

Sleep feels futile, so I get out of bed and throw on a sports bra and hoodie. I don't think about my chest most days, but sometimes I'm too aware of it, especially on these late-night QuikMart runs; the weight, the way Terry's eyes immediately go there.

Gram's asleep in front of the TV when I tiptoe past her, though I know she wouldn't try to stop me even if she was awake. I've been doing these late-night bike rides since I was fourteen.

She hated it at first. But I knew the world was dangerous. I didn't need her to remind me.

"Sid."

Fuck. She's not asleep.

"Gram," I say.

She doesn't ask where I'm going. She never does.

I look at her. She looks older than she is; she just turned sixty-four last year. Had my dad and his sisters young.

They don't talk to her anymore. Not since Dad was arrested.

I don't get it. She didn't defend him. She and I both know what he did, and it's not like she's tried to pretend her son was a perfect angel who'd never commit a crime in his life. She didn't even ask the judge for leniency at his sentencing.

Then again, maybe that's why Dad's sisters don't visit. If a woman throws her only son under the bus like that, what would she do to her daughters?

"How'd the search go?"

"Fine," I say. "I don't think we're gonna find her alive. It's been four days."

Gram sighs. But she doesn't disagree with me. I'm almost to the door when she stops me.

"You know your daddy didn't do it."

I stop. I don't need her to tell me that, but all I can think about is the fact June's head was shaved. That dad may not have killed the girls this time, but someone's killing them now because of him.

That this is still, always, his fault.

"I know, Gram."

She stares me straight in the eyes. "I know you think you're invincible 'cause you're young and you ain't a girl and you've grown up with evil. But someone's out there targeting girls. I'm not gonna stop you from going out and riding, but . . . be careful, okay?"

I nod. "Yeah. Okay, Gram."

What else am I supposed to say to her? This is the most we've acknowledged what he did in years. It's not like I'm going to argue with her and tell her I don't need to be careful.

I'm almost out the door when she speaks again. "And Sid?"

"Yeah?"

"Plain pork rinds this time, please. Not the barbecue ones."

My bike's leaning against the wall of our trailer. It's not locked. I don't know where I want to start riding. I just want the exercise, the ability to get away from here and not be trapped in my own head. I'll have to stop at the gas station at some point, but for now?

For now I just want to get out. Besides, if I stay home I'll have nothing to think about but the ghosts. Lauren, June, whoever.

You're really good at making our deaths about you, *aren't you?*

I can't think about that right now. So I ride. Down back roads and through the woods for a while before I get too spooked, taking the long way to the convenience store. My legs burn, and my chest aches and I can't catch my breath, but I have to keep going.

I try not to look at Savannah's billboard as I round the last corner before the gas station. Try not to think about all the missing girls in this town, all the names on billboards and coffee cans.

Who's paying for the billboard, I wonder. Is it Savannah's family? June's? Someone who doesn't even know them but wants to help?

One of Dad's victims' families? The family of a girl who didn't get a billboard of her own?

I've never talked to any of them. Most of them moved away after Dad was sentenced. Only Melissa Wagner and Dawn Schaefer's families stuck around, but as far as I know, they both live on the other side of the county.

I hate him. I hate him for killing those girls and I hate him for what's happening now, because he's the cause of it even if he's not actively involved.

He's my dad, and I love him and I hate him and living with that is the hardest thing I do.

The lottery numbers are lit up again in the convenience store when I finally make it there—different ones, this week.

Maybe I should buy a ticket. Doesn't the universe fucking owe me? Wouldn't that balance things out?

Terry's got his earbuds in when I walk in, and again he's the only one in there. The scraggly hair on his face is longer.

I grab what I need, including a box of pads, and head to the counter. June's photo has been replaced on the Folgers can by Savannah's.

Have You Seen This Girl?

Terry hands me my cigarettes. I ignore whatever smart comment he makes about Savannah.

I wish the ghosts would bother him. He's more of a creep than I am. Never mind his dad didn't kill them. His brother, Johnny, was a suspect for a long time until his alibis cleared him; both brothers denied even knowing my dad.

Dad never mentioned anything about him, though. . . .

But Dad didn't mention a lot of things. What if he just didn't want to admit he had help?

Paranoia shoots through my chest. I haven't seen Johnny lately, but I have seen Terry—

I shouldn't think that. He's a creep, but he's not a killer.

"That's what you need to find out, Sidney," June whispers in my ear. I whip around, but she's not there.

"Leave me alone," I hiss.

Terry looks up at me. "What'd you say?"

His gaze travels down to my chest and back up, deliberately, and I cross my arms.

"Nothing," I mutter, and grab my cigarettes and chips and pork rinds and pads and head out the door.

◆ ◆ ◆

I am not a girl.

It's what they told me from birth I was, and I believed them for a long time.

But it started to feel more and more wrong in recent years. The word *girl* just doesn't fit me. When I think about myself, I don't think *girl*. I don't think *boy*, either. I just think Sid. I just am.

There are words for me, but what would be the point? No one here would get them, and it's not like I want to make it this big thing when it isn't. When I don't have any feelings about it, no heavy thoughts. I'm just Sid. I'm neither.

But this town's never going to see me that way, so why bother.

But Mavis. God, it's nice to have someone see me as I actually want to be seen.

I think about her again. Her hand in mine and her laughter and the way she asked about my pronouns and the way she looks at me.

My bike wheel bounces and I look up, realizing I've drifted off the road onto the shoulder. I keep riding that way, anyway, because it makes me pay attention.

And then a flash of red illuminated by the streetlamp catches my eye, and I pull my bike over and skid to a stop, the plastic bag of snacks and cigarettes falling off my bike handle.

The red is a piece of fabric. A zip-up jacket with a faded label.

My hands shake as I reach for the jacket before I snatch them back. I don't want to touch it, just in case. Who leaves a jacket out on the side of the road?

God, I hate to think it, but it'd be really fucking helpful right now if Savannah just showed up and told me this was hers.

"Not how it works, babe."

It's June.

"Go away. I found something. Isn't this what you want?"

"You found it too late."

I look up, and I almost scream. I can see her clearly now. June. Her head is shaved. She's starting to decompose, her skin sloughing off her cheeks, peeling off her arms.

"Fuck you," I retort. "I didn't ask for this."

"You think I asked for this?" she snarls, gesturing to her body, her head, the bones starting to peek through flesh. "No one asks for it."

"I don't even know where to start looking."

She laughs. "Think like a killer, Sid."

"I—"

"What, you don't know how? Why don't you go ask your dad?"

"He didn't kill you," I say, but my voice shakes.

"He might as well have," she snaps. "And he knows how they think." She taps her temple with a bony finger and then leans down, her fingers ghosting over the jacket. "Talk to him. Find out. Or I'm just going to keep coming back, and I'll bring the rest of them with me, and we won't leave you alone until you find us."

"Why me?"

She looks at me. "You know why," she says, and disappears.

I call the anonymous tip line for crime, report the jacket.

And then I ride home, hands shaking so much I can barely steer my bike.

I wish I could text Mavis. Call her. I wish I had someone to talk to about this since I can't talk to Gram.

But telling Mavis about the ghosts would mean admitting that I think they're real. And I can't do that, either. What the fuck does June want, anyway? Photos taped to my wall connected with red string?

How does she expect me to solve this?

I fall asleep, and I'm still thinking about that fucking red jacket.

I think Red Riding Hood got eaten by the wolves.

Savannah Baunach: January 16, 2018

A GIRL walks home through the woods from her boyfriend's house. It's a shortcut she's taken several times before.

She knows what happened to June. She just attended her funeral a few hours before.

But a girl shouldn't have to be scared in her own neighborhood.

She thinks about her boyfriend. Craig. He's nice enough. As boys go.

He likes her a lot more than she likes him, though. And she knows it. She can tell by how he touches her, shy and fumbling when she just wants to take his hands and put them where she wants.

(She isn't supposed to want that, though. She's supposed to want him shy and fumbling and unsure.)

(She isn't supposed to want him at all. Not until there's a ring on her finger and she's got his last name instead of hers.)

Her mother doesn't know about Craig.

Savannah wants to keep it that way.

She cuts through trees and branches. The streetlights are on, and she can see her house in the distance.

She wonders what she'll tell her mother. Maybe that a few of the girls wanted to meet up after the funeral, Kate and the rest. She feels a twinge of guilt, using June as an excuse like that, and it grows when she thinks about the fact that maybe she should have been doing that instead, instead of being with Craig.

But she didn't want to think about the fact her best friend was dead, just for a few hours, and she thinks June might have understood that.

She pulls her phone out of her pocket, sends a quick text to Kate asking if they can get breakfast early tomorrow morning and cram for their chemistry exam.

When a hand closes over her mouth, she's too surprised to scream.

She drops her phone, doesn't see where it lands.

Her mother made her take self-defense classes, but all she remembers is something about going for the eyes, and she can't reach whoever's grabbing her, not his eyes, and any other knowledge she had flies out of her head because there is a hand wrapped around her throat and the world goes

Dark.

Chapter Six

THINGS STAY relatively quiet until Thursday, and I've almost let myself forget about the jacket. It's warm as I bike to school, too warm for January. I debate taking my hoodie off as I pull into the school parking lot, but all I have on under it is an old T-shirt. Besides, it'll be cold again inside; the heat's been broken in our English classroom since last year.

I park my bike in the far corner of the lot, away from the parents dropping their kids off at the entrance. More and more parents have been doing that since Savannah disappeared, not wanting their kids to drive alone. Especially the girls.

None of them would offer me a ride, I know; none of them would tell me I shouldn't bike because it isn't safe out here. To them I'm just another reminder that it isn't.

"Sid!"

I turn. Sally Louise is hurrying toward me, her keys dangling from her hand. She, at least, drove herself, but who's going to kidnap the sheriff's daughter?

"Can I talk to you?" she asks. "In private?"

"Sure," I say. My heart skips a beat. Maybe she has more information on June, or Savannah, more confirmation that someone's copying Dad. Or maybe she'll tell me it's all just a coincidence, that Savannah's been found safe, that what happened ten years ago has nothing to do with what's happening now.

But I know that's just wishful thinking.

Sally Louise leads me over to the side of the building, the part that stretches out into a bare lot where our teachers sometimes come out for smoke breaks, though they'd never admit that if asked.

"What's up?"

"Dad said he got an anonymous tip Saturday night about a jacket," Sally Louise says, and I work very hard to keep my expression neutral. "I wanted to see if you knew anything about it."

"Why would I know anything about that?"

"Because he says they found it near that gas station you ride your bike to sometimes," she says. "I know where you live, remember?"

"Creepy," I say, unable to stop myself, and she glares at me.

"Be serious."

"I am being serious. I don't know anything about a jacket." I don't break her gaze. Between the two of us, I've always been the better liar. "Is it Savannah's?"

"It's too big," Sally Louise says. I tamp the relief down. "I mean, he's not ruling it out."

"Good idea," I say, and she rolls her eyes.

"You're sure you don't know anything about it?"

"I'm sure," I say. Sally Louise gives me that look that says she doesn't quite believe me, but she doesn't push it.

"Well," she finally says, tucking a piece of hair behind her ear, "if you do have any idea who called it in, let me know. Dad might want to question them."

"Will do," I say, and I hang back so she can walk into the building, just so we aren't seen together.

It's more for her sake than for mine.

Things stay relatively quiet most of the day until third period civics, when Craig is called to the office. Everyone else immediately breaks out into frantic whispers.

The jacket was too big to be Savannah's. What if it's Craig's?

But Craig was out looking for her, surely he wouldn't—

"Your dad looked for us, too," Alicia Graves hisses in my ear, and I hunch my shoulders up farther as if that'll block out the sound of her voice.

By calculus, my last period of the day, the rumors about Craig have only intensified. Someone says they saw him acting weird the day after Savannah disappeared, but they won't say what acting weird means. Someone says he left the search for her after only five minutes. Someone *else* says that Craig stuck next to the sheriff the entire time, not to help but to deliberately lead him away from where he'd hidden Savannah. Someone briefly suggests that Craig did this because he and Jenny are secretly fucking, but that gets dismissed quickly. Rumors about Craig are one thing. Rumors about Savannah's sister are another entirely.

Mr. Sheffield, our calculus teacher, has given up on telling us to be quiet. He'd declared it a free period at the start of class as long as we worked on something from our textbooks and as long as we kept our mouths shut, but both of those things quickly got ignored, and he didn't bother trying to get us back on track. He keeps glancing between Craig and Savannah's empty seats. I'm sure he's got his own theories, the way everyone else does.

Only Mavis, Sally Louise, and I haven't contributed to the gossip. Mavis has been reading *Jane Eyre*, seemingly oblivious to everyone else, and I've given up entirely and put my head on my desk. Sally keeps shooting looks at Lilah Crenshaw like she wants her to shut up, but she hasn't actually said anything to her yet, either.

"I heard Craig was pissed because Savannah got into ECU, and he got waitlisted," Alison Woods says.

"Please," Lilah says. "We all know that's not true. Craig's been saying he wanted to go to UNC since, like, August. Besides, he didn't kill Savannah. That's bullshit."

"Language, Miss Crenshaw," Mr. Sheffield says tiredly.

"Sorry. Anyway. Craig didn't do it." Lilah's gaze fixes on me, and her face twists into something ugly. "If anyone here killed Savannah, it's Sid."

"I didn't hurt Savannah." I can't bring myself to say kill. Lilah notices.

"I said you probably killed her, not that you *hurt* her," she says. "I thought you'd know the difference, what with your dad and all."

"Fuck you," I snap.

"Language, Miss Crane—"

"That's not my name," I snarl, turning to Mr. Sheffield, who's gone white at his own mistake. He knows it. I know it.

"I bet she did do it," Lilah stage-whispers, and I whip around to face her, ignore the knife in my chest at *she*. "Bet her daddy taught her how. Rotten like that runs in the family, my mama says."

No one says anything. No one comes to my defense. Even Sally Louise just grimaces at me. I look around desperately, hoping for someone to say something, anything, to disagree with her, but no one does.

My eyes finally land on Mavis. She's looking at me, too, but not with shock. With disappointment. With pity.

She knew. She already knew.

"Sid . . . ," she begins, but the bell rings, and I'm saved from having to hear anything she has to say, gathering my stuff and running out the door before anyone can stop me, Lilah Crenshaw's words still ringing in my ears.

"Sid! Sid, just wait!"

Mavis finds me by the fire exit near the art room, her face red when she reaches me. She has to fight through the crowd of students to get to me. A few of them glance our way, but I ignore it, and soon enough the hallway is empty. No one wants to be caught here late anymore.

"What do you want, Mavis?" I ask.

"Please, I just want to talk to you—"

"I don't want to talk to you," I snap, trying hard to not react to the hurt that flashes across her face when I do. "Leave me alone."

"Sid . . ."

"Please," I say. She sighs, but she doesn't leave.

I don't dare get my hopes up at that.

"Who told you?" I ask after a minute, when it's become clear she isn't going anywhere, because if she's going to make me talk to her, I'm at least going to get answers. "About . . . about my dad?"

About the girls?

LAUREN O'MALLEY
ALICIA GRAVES
MELISSA WAGNER
DAWN SCHAEFER
SAMANTHA MARKHAM
~~JUNE HARGROVE~~
~~SAVANNAH BAUNACH~~

There are icy fingers on my shoulder. I don't bother to turn around. I know it's June. Mavis's eyes widen. For a second I wonder if she can see her, too, but when I turn, June is gone. And Mavis is staring at me like there was nothing there in the first place.

"Lilah told me," she says. "The day of June's funeral, after you and I met at the diner. She—she came up to me when you left and asked if I knew who you were, and why would I be hanging out with someone like you?" She laughs bitterly.

She knew. That's the one thought running through my mind right now. She knew already. Mavis. I'd been so worried about her finding out and she . . .

"You knew," I say, and it comes out shaky. "You . . . you knew and you still spent time with me—"

"I was waiting for you to tell me," she says. "I thought you might, after the assembly for Savannah, or during the search—"

"How? How was I supposed to tell you that, Mavis? When

would it have been the right time for me to say, 'Hey, I know we're searching for this missing girl and by the way, did you know my dad is a serial killer and he killed five girls, too?'" I wipe at my eyes furiously. "You—you let me think that you didn't know, you let me believe I could actually *have* something with you."

"Because I wanted *you* to tell me, Sid," she says. "It's not my fucking place to ask who your dad is, or what he did, especially since Savannah went missing. I didn't want to remind you—"

"Didn't want to remind me? Fuck, Mavis, girls are going missing *because of him*."

She steps back at that, her face paling. "You don't know that. It could just be a coincidence."

"It's not," I say hollowly. "I know it's not. Sally told me. June's head was shaved, when she was found. It's what—it's what he did." I can't call him my dad. Not now. "When he killed girls. He always . . . shaved their heads."

I can't look at her. I want her to go away, but she isn't. She's just standing there while I confirm every awful thing my dad did, and for a second it's not June's hand I feel on my shoulder, but his.

"Why did you try to hide it from me?" she asks after a minute.

Because I didn't want you to look at me the way you're looking at me now.

"Because," I say, and I feel like I'm about to cry and I hate it.

"Because for once in my life I wanted someone to know me for me, and not for what my dad did. I—I gave up, down here, at having any sort of friends or connection or anything because of *him*, and then you come along and you don't—you didn't know what he did and you didn't look at me like you hated me and you asked about my *pronouns* and . . ." My voice breaks.

I can't cry about this, though. I haven't since the day Dad was sentenced. I'm not going to now.

"Sid . . ."

"Leave me alone," I say again, and this time when I push past her she doesn't try to follow me. I leave her standing there and wish, more than anything, that I didn't.

Because all I can picture is that expression on her face that I've seen on everyone else's in this town a thousand times over, that expression that says no matter how hard I try, people are only ever going to look at me and see Dennis Crane's daughter.

I can hear the muffled sounds of the TV through the screen door even as I'm walking up to the trailer, and I pray that Gram's only watching reruns of Billy Engel and not watching the news. There was a reporter in the parking lot when I left school and I did my best to avoid her, hood up, earbuds in, biking like my life depended on it. I don't think she spotted me.

But the cadences of a TV preacher are unmistakable, and that's what I hear as I open the door, and I breathe a sigh of relief. I drop my backpack by the door with a *thump*, harder than intended, and Gram turns her head.

She doesn't ask if I had a rough day. Doesn't ask how school was. I want so badly to curl up in her lap like I would have if I was a kid, back when I still went by my full name and she was just the grandmother I visited for the holidays.

I can't do that anymore. I want to tell her about Mavis, about Lilah, but I don't want that pitying look I got from her the last time I told her I didn't really have any friends. The one time she asked.

"I'm gonna go do homework," I say instead, and I pick up my backpack and make my way down the hall to my room, making sure to shut the door softly behind me. I flop down on my bed, half-heartedly thinking about actually doing homework. Not that it's going to matter. Not like any of our teachers are checking to see if anything's done, anyway. Mrs. Hill is the only one making any sort of attempt at trying to keep us on a schedule, and that's only because she wants to get the book done before we go on spring break. We're supposed to decide on a theme to analyze in pairs by then, too.

Thinking about *Jane Eyre* makes me think about Mavis, which just makes my chest hurt.

"Sucks, doesn't it?"

I sit up, half expecting to see June perched on the edge of my bed. But it isn't June. It's Lauren O'Malley, and my blood runs cold.

I've never seen Lauren before. I only know it's her because

she looks like her senior yearbook portrait, the one that ran in the newspapers for a week after her disappearance.

Have You Seen This Girl?

I wonder about the logic of that, June rotting away while Lauren gets to look alive. But I shouldn't be wondering at all. All she's ever been is a voice. She can't be real. Not like June is real.

But I'm seeing Lauren now, so what does that mean?

"*I'm* not real?" she says, and her voice is a far-off echo. "You're the one who's barely here." She smiles, and it's then I see the rot, half her teeth missing.

"Go away."

"No." She laughs, inching closer, and wraps an arm around my shoulder like we're best friends. Her touch is cold, dripping wet, water settling into the crook of my elbow, falling down the back of my shirt.

"It sucks, doesn't it?" she whispers again in my ear. "Only being known for your dad. How do you think *we* feel?"

And then all of them are there, sitting on the edge of my bed, these girls whose pictures I know from newspaper articles and memorials in our high school. Lauren, Alicia, Melissa, Dawn, Samantha. Their fingers dig into my arms, my legs, pinning me to my bed.

"Your father is the most interesting thing about us," one of them hisses in my ear. "Do you know how that feels?"

"I—"

"Shh," Lauren says, putting a cold finger up to my lips, and I gasp.

"You deserve to be alone," one of them says—Melissa, I think. "You deserve to know how we feel."

"You think I don't know how you feel?" I snap, thinking of Mavis, of Lilah, of the whole damn town.

Lauren screams. Her jaw pops, opening wider than I thought it could have, and I can't cover my ears because all of them are holding me down.

"At least," she snarls at me, "you're still *alive*."

And then they're gone, as quickly as they appeared, and I'm left gasping for air like I'm drowning, like how they felt in their last moments before my father killed them.

The first time someone outside our town recognized me in public, I was fifteen. Gram and I had driven out to Raleigh for new school supplies. It was only my second summer living with her and we were both still so new to it, her having to care for a teenager and me living with more supervision. Gram was stricter than Dad had been, since he hadn't been around much, and I was constantly pushing, trying to see what I could get away with with her.

We were in the clearance section at Roses Discount Store. My hair was down. I'd cut it just the week before, and it fell just below my ears. I was arguing with Gram, who was trying to convince me to try on a purple blouse. I liked purple. I didn't like the ruffles on the blouse. Already I was beginning to feel itchy in my skin, in my girlhood, but I didn't have a name for that feeling yet. The only feeling I had a name for was that I didn't want to wear something with ruffles.

"Marybeth Crane? Is that you?"

At my father's last name, Gram stiffened. We both turned. The voice belonged to an older white woman, maybe Gram's age. Her hair was an unnatural red color that clashed with her skin, and what I remember most is that she had long fingernails painted a bright, garish yellow.

Gram didn't correct her on her last name. We'd changed it back to her maiden one, Atkinson, only a few weeks before.

"That's me," Gram said, her tone wary, and then the woman's attention turned to me.

"And this must be Sidney. Goodness, she does look just like her father."

"Do I know you?" Gram said, her voice cold. The woman faltered from where she'd been bending down to touch me, but she tried to smile at Gram.

"Of course you do, Marybeth. I sat behind you at Our Lady of Sorrows for fifteen years."

This time I frowned. Gram was Baptist, even if she didn't practice much anymore.

The woman reached out for me again and this time she

succeeded, fingering the ends of my hair. "Such a tragedy, what happened with Dennis, though it's nice to see you're holding up—"

Gram swatted her hand away at the same time I recoiled.

"We're not Catholic. Never have been," Gram said shortly, and before I could react she had grabbed my hand and was pulling me out of the store, the ruffled blouse forgotten on the sale rack.

"Who was that?" I asked as we got in the car.

Gram's jaw set. "I ain't never met that woman in my life," she said. "Some busybody who thinks she knows who we are just because she's seen your daddy on the news, tryin' to pretend like we're friends so she can take some gossip home to her family."

She took the highway home faster than I had ever seen her drive. The next day she changed our phone number. A week later she'd sent in the paperwork to hide her address from public records.

And when we got home, I closed myself in the bathroom with a pair of clippers. I didn't know what I was doing, not really. All I knew was that I didn't want someone to be able to touch me like that again.

Gram never said anything. Not when she came in the bathroom to half of my hair on the floor. Not when she picked up the clippers herself and finished the back of my head that I couldn't reach. She just dug around in the closet and gave me an old beanie to wear to school, and that was the end of that.

I've cut my own hair ever since. Tried as hard as I can to make sure no one calls either of us by Dad's last name.

But it won't work. No matter how much my appearance changes, no matter how much the newspapers promised not to publish my name since I was a minor. All anyone in this town is ever going to see when they look at me is Dad.

Alicia Graves: January 16, 2008

ALICIA GRAVES was the second girl my father killed. She wasn't found until after he'd already killed Melissa. I don't know if it's because her dad waited a few days to even bother reporting her missing, or if the sheriff's department was too small to put much of an effort in, or simply if no one cared.

Her mom had died of cancer the year before. Her dad, according to a few articles, was drinking or absent most of the time. He died the year my dad was arrested, in February. He never knew who killed his daughter.

People will say he would've drank himself to death either way, that that's the path he was headed down regardless, but I don't know.

I think what my dad did might have killed him, too.

A girl finishes her shift at the Piggly Wiggly earlier than she's supposed to. She's mopped the floors twice, just to have something to do, just so she doesn't have to walk out to her car alone.

Stalling while she waits for Johnny to count the money in the back, since he promised to walk her out to her car.

Normally she wouldn't take him up on it. No girl wants to be alone with Johnny Pritchard, but she figures between Lauren O'Malley's disappearance or being alone with Johnny, he's the lesser of two evils.

Besides, she knows it can't be him. Lauren went missing a week ago, when Alicia and Johnny both had a shift at the Piggly Wiggly. She remembers because he made some comment about her sweatshirt and how tight it was, and she hasn't worn it since despite the fact it's her favorite.

She leans against the mop before wiping her forehead and pulling her long dark hair into a ponytail. She goes to bang on the door of the manager's office, the radio playing faintly behind it.

"Hurry up," she says. Normally she's nicer to Johnny, but she's in no mood right now, it's cold and she just wants to get home.

"Just a minute," he says. "Don't get your panties in a knot." She hears his laugh ring out from behind the door, ugly and braying, and she shudders.

Maybe she will just walk out to her car alone. Can't be worse than having to put up with Johnny.

"I'm going to leave if you don't hurry up," she says. She can see her car, parked under one of the streetlamps, the orange glow throwing into sharp relief just how banged up it really is.

Not like she can afford a new one. Not like anyone in this town can, except maybe Sheriff Lee.

She wonders what he's doing with his time. If he's trying to find Lauren or if he's just bumming around with her dad again.

It takes another two minutes, but she finally gets fed up, worrying more now about being here alone with Johnny than she is about walking to her car.

"Look, I'll see you tomorrow," she calls through the door, and grabs her backpack from the lockers in the back before heading out the front entrance. Johnny'll lock up, and she'll get shit from her supervisor tomorrow about not staying, but she doesn't care. She just wants to go home.

There's only one other car in the parking lot besides Johnny's truck, one as old and beat-up as hers. The hairs on the back of her neck stand up, but the car's parked far enough from her own. It's too dark to see if anyone's in it, but probably not; probably it's just abandoned for the day and the owner will come get it tomorrow, or it'll be towed.

She unlocks her car and tosses her backpack into the backseat, then walks around to the driver's side. There's something wrong with the door so she has to manually unlock it, and she fumbles with her keys for a few seconds.

A hand clamps over her mouth before she's even fully inserted the key. For a minute she worries it's Johnny, but she knows it isn't; she hadn't seen him come outside.

She tries to bite, but there's a cloth pressed to her nose now, chemical and strange, and she breathes it in.

Her last thought is if her dad will even notice if she doesn't come home.

Chapter Seven

ALL WEEKEND, I bury myself in trying to find any concrete evidence about Savannah's disappearance. But there's no new information; the cops are being more tight-lipped than ever. Just the same article I've already read from the day she was reported missing.

The cops withholding information doesn't stop the rumors from continuing to grow, though. The story about the jacket possibly being Savannah's has already stretched into something bizarre and grotesque—now it's not an anonymous tip but the killer himself who reported it, calling in to gloat.

I'm more thankful than ever that no one knows it was me who called it in.

But still. That doesn't stop everyone from avoiding me on Monday regardless, giving me a wide berth in the halls like I'm suddenly going to lash out and strangle them. Even the teachers act like I'm not there. Only Sally Louise looks mildly sympathetic, but even that feels superficial.

I avoid Mavis entirely.

She keeps texting me. I keep ignoring them. The last one she sent Saturday just says:

I'm here if you want to talk.

But I don't know what I'd say to her. By the beginning of fourth period I wish they'd just let us out early again, since it's not like any of us are getting any work done. Even during calculus, the one class I try to pay attention during, Mr. Sheffield just has us practice equations from the book. Mavis's head is bowed in front of me.

Like in the other classes we have together, she's in June's seat.

I should stop thinking of it as June's seat.

There are more empty seats now, including Lilah's—parents keeping their kids home, most likely. Mrs. Crenshaw has always been overprotective, though I can't say I'm not grateful to not have to deal with Lilah. Her laughter isn't following me down the halls, and Sally Louise looks slightly lost without her, though we both know it's always been Lilah who's needed her, and not the other way around.

The sick feeling in my stomach, though, only grows. Something feels wrong. Something *is* wrong.

There's a knock on our door then, and Mr. Sheffield glances at it before looking back at us, like we're supposed to know what to do. He opens the door, and there stands Sheriff Kepler.

The whispers increase in volume immediately. If Sheriff

Kepler is here, that can only mean something's happening with the disappearances.

Sally Louise starts to stand, but the sheriff holds up a hand, and she sits back in her seat.

"Sidney Atkinson?" he asks. Every head turns at his words as I stand up, fighting the urge to pull my hood over my head.

"Sir?"

"I need you to come with me, Sidney," he says, and I wince at the use of my full name again, one that no one uses for me anymore except for Lilah when she wants to get under my skin. I've been Sid since the day I took those clippers to my hair.

"Did I do something, sir?" I ask, knowing that even asking him is a bad idea, feels like a bad idea, because I know that's what everyone's thinking right now. But I feel like I have to say something, even if it's just to drown out everyone else's whispers.

"Just come with me," he says, and I gather my stuff, knocking my math book off my desk in my hurry. No one stoops to help me with it, and I awkwardly bend down and shove it into my backpack before following the sheriff out the door.

I know everyone's staring at me. I don't have to look back.

As soon as we get into the hallway I pull my hood over my head. When Sheriff Kepler and I exit the school, there are more news vans circling the parking lot. I pull my hood tighter, praying they're not filming, but we all know journalistic integrity has never really meant anything around here.

And if they knew who I was, any remaining integrity they had would fly out the window if it meant they'd get an exclusive with Dennis Crane's daughter.

Sheriff Kepler guides me to his car, and I thank god it's an unmarked one, because the last thing I need right now is to be driven out of here in the back of a cop car.

"What's this about?" I ask, but he just turns the radio on to some country station Gram loves and I hate. I keep quiet until we pull into the station, terror filling me the closer we get. Something has happened to Gram. Someone has killed my father. They know I called in the jacket.

They think I killed the girls.

We get out of the car and I wordlessly follow him into the station.

For a second I think we're going to go to his office, but we don't. Instead he leads me into a windowless room, and my heart begins to beat faster because I know what this is.

It's an interrogation. Of course.

"Can I get you a water?" he asks, and it's so cliché that the urge to laugh bubbles up in me before I stuff it back down and shake my head. He sighs, taking the seat opposite mine.

"Shouldn't Gram be here if you're going to question me?"

"Do you want Marybeth to come down here?" he asks, and I shake my head no. "Besides. This isn't formal. We're just talking."

I press my lips tight together. I know enough not to say anything else.

"You wanted to know why you're here?" he asks, and I nod, because I at least want to know that. After a minute he seems to realize that I'm not going to say anything else, and he sighs. "Lilah Crenshaw didn't come home Friday night."

Shock must register across my face, because he leans back in his chair and looks at me. "That news to you, Sidney?"

I take a breath. This feels like some cop show, some late-night thing that would come on after Gram fell asleep in front of the television. A rotating cast of suspects, but the cops are always, always the good guys. And they always catch whoever did it in less than an hour.

Sheriff Kepler and I both know that isn't how it works, though.

SHERIFF KEPLER: *[drumming his fingers on his desk.]* Do you know what I'm about to ask you?

[Beat.]

SHERIFF KEPLER: A few witnesses told me they saw you fighting with Lilah Crenshaw on Thursday afternoon. Some of your classmates.

SID: It wasn't a fight.

[SHERIFF KEPLER leans back in his chair.]

SHERIFF KEPLER: That’s not what I heard. Why don’t you set the record straight for me?

SID: She was just . . . saying I had something to do with it. With the girls going missing. Because of my dad.

SHERIFF KEPLER: Do you?

SID: No.

[Beat.]

SID *[more emphatically]*: No, I don’t. Shouldn’t you—shouldn’t you be questioning Craig about this?

SHERIFF KEPLER: I shouldn’t discuss other suspects with you, but Craig Hutchens has an alibi for the night Savannah went missing, and the night June Hargrove disappeared. He was at home Sunday night when Lilah went missing; both parents confirmed that.

SID: Have you—have you looked at Terry or Johnny Pritchard?

SHERIFF KEPLER: Why would I do that?

SID: The jacket was found near their store, wasn’t it?

SHERIFF KEPLER: How would you know that, Sidney?

[Beat.]

SHERIFF KEPLER: I was wondering who would've made that call. You do ride your bike a lot out there. Several of my boys have said they see you around late at night. One of them almost hit you with a car last year, you know? Need to start wearing some brighter clothes.

SID: Was there a question in that?

SHERIFF KEPLER: No, Sidney. No question.

SID: Reporting the jacket doesn't mean I—it doesn't mean I know what happened.

SHERIFF KEPLER: Let's try this again. Do you know where Lilah Crenshaw is? Did you have anything to do with her disappearance?

SID: No.

SHERIFF KEPLER: Do you think your father has something to do with this?

SID: Don't see how he could.

SHERIFF KEPLER: No one he's in contact with on the outside? Mighty big coincidence that girls are getting killed the exact same dates they did ten years ago, don't you think?

SID: Johnny Pritchard was questioned last time—

SHERIFF KEPLER: Johnny Pritchard isn't under suspicion now.

[Beat.]

SHERIFF KEPLER: I want to catch who's doing this, Sidney. I think you do too. But I can't if you don't help me.

SID: I don't know anything.

SHERIFF KEPLER: I don't believe that.

SID: I didn't know anything last time, either. I was a *kid*.

SHERIFF KEPLER: We're not talking about last time. We're talking about now. Don't you want to help me? Don't you want this town to stop pointing fingers at you for a crime you didn't commit?

SID: So now I *don't* have anything to do with it?

SHERIFF KEPLER: Don't get smart with me, Crane.

[SID flinches.]

SHERIFF KEPLER: Fine. If you won't tell me anything to save your own skin, maybe you'll do it for Lilah. I know the two of you didn't always get along, from what Sally tells me—girls your age are always fighting about one thing or another—

SID: I'm not a girl.

SHERIFF KEPLER: Whatever you are then, Sidney Crane.

SID: My last name is Atkinson.

SHERIFF KEPLER: Right. Of course. Sidney Atkinson.

SID: Sid.

SHERIFF KEPLER: *Sid* Atkinson. You don't know where Lilah is, then?

SID: No. I don't.

SHERIFF KEPLER: I hate to ask this, but I'm going to, and I'm only going to ask it once because I don't want to put this on a teenage girl—teenager. Did you kill June Hargrove?

[Silence.]

SHERIFF KEPLER: Do you know who took her? Savannah Baunach?

[Silence.]

SHERIFF KEPLER: Have you seen Lilah Crenshaw? Does your father have anything to do with the disappearance of these girls?

[Silence.]

[Silence.]

[Silence.]

Sheriff Kepler lets me go after an hour, after it's clear I don't have anything else to say. I want to tell him I'd help him if I could.

Maybe I should have told him about the ghosts. Maybe if I had, they'd bother him instead of me, point him toward finding something—though with how unhelpful they've been to me, I know it wouldn't happen.

What my head is still spinning with is what Sheriff Kepler said. *Girls are getting killed the exact same dates they did ten years ago.* So whoever's doing this really is copying my dad.

I keep my suspicions to myself, though. Can't trust a cop, not ever, not even one I know.

I excuse myself to find a bathroom, and when I return Sally Louise is sitting at the sheriff's desk, her eyes red. I wonder how she got there before remembering that it was last period when the sheriff called me out. School must be over.

Seeing Sally Louise in this office, in this space, just makes the knife of memory poke at my ribs, because I used to hang out here with her when I was younger.

Way before they arrested Dad, way before he was under any sort of suspicion. I was nine, and Sally Louise and I would play with her Barbies on the floor of the sheriff's office.

I remember being jealous of Sally Louise, though I was always jealous of her back then, even if I felt special because she let me call her just "Sally" when no one else got that privilege except her family. She was always dressed nicer than I was at school, with newer clothes that I couldn't even dream of having.

Gram brought me home a dress once from Goodwill before I stopped wearing them and I knew it had been Sally Louise's, because I'd seen her wear it to school two months before. It was plaid, with small butterflies embroidered around the hem in sparkly thread so they looked like they were in motion, and I knew that as much as I loved that dress I could never wear it to school, never, because she would know. And maybe she wouldn't have said anything about it, but maybe she would have. Maybe someone else would have, and she would have had to join in.

The sheriff sees her and awkwardly clears his throat before mumbling something about having left his keys in the back room.

Sally finally looks at me. And for a second the ghost I see out of the corner of my eye isn't June Hargrove, but me and Sally at nine, our laughter so loud it can't even be contained by this office.

She was nice to me. That's what I remember most. Before we found out what my dad had done. She let me play with her Barbies, much nicer than the knockoffs I had, and we made up elaborate storylines with them that had nothing to do with murder but that were bigger than us, bigger than where we lived. Even then I could tell—she was going to be something bigger than this town.

She didn't talk to me after Dad was arrested. She didn't even keep me company whenever I had to come by the sheriff's office. I don't know if that was Sheriff Kepler's idea, or hers. I don't think I'll ask her.

I cannot let her turn into one of the ghosts that haunts me and follows me around.

"Sid," she says, standing up from where she's been sitting at her father's desk like maybe she's about to offer me the seat, but she doesn't. When she looks at me, her eyes are hard. There's no trace of the girl she was.

There's no trace of the girl I was though, either.

"Hey," I say, and we both stand there awkwardly, looking at each other. I wonder if she's remembering the same things I am.

"I didn't think you'd still be here."

"Yeah, well. Your dad had a lot of questions," I say. She nods, and I feel compelled to add, "I don't know, by the way . . . what happened to Lilah. I haven't—haven't seen her."

"I didn't think you had," Sally says. She sighs. "But of course I didn't get to tell Dad that." She bites her lip, and she looks so much like him in that instant that it chills me.

Do I look that much like my own father?

"I just—I just need to grab my stuff," I say, and without a

word she hands me my backpack. We both know her dad isn't coming back for a minute.

"You'll want to go out the back way," Sally says. "News vans are out front. I don't think you want them to see you."

I nod. Shift my backpack to my other shoulder. "I . . . my bike's at school. Your dad drove me here."

"Huh," she says, just as Sheriff Kepler takes that moment to reappear. "I guess you're getting a ride home with us, then." She looks at her dad for confirmation; he just nods.

"So this means I'm not under suspicion?" I ask, and both Keplers turn to look at me. Sally looks amused. Her dad looks angry.

"For now," he says. I start to follow them, but he holds up a hand. "But if I found out you haven't told me anything . . ."

"I'll share whatever new information I find with you, Sheriff," I deadpan, and his face colors. Sally Louise tries not to smile.

"This isn't a joke, Crane," he says, but I don't flinch at the name this time.

"I know it's not," I say. I don't need him to tell me that, not ever. Sally looks at me, and I think the sheriff is just going to let me have the last word, because without another one he strides out to his car, leaving us to follow behind.

The sheriff drops Sally Louise off first before he takes me home. I don't ask if he can stop at school for my bike. He's already doing me a favor, and maybe Gram will be able to drive me tomorrow.

Sally didn't say a word to me when she got out of the car, just gave me a look, and I wondered if she was thinking about all the times I ever went to her house, or if she was just thinking about Lilah.

Sheriff Kepler makes his way toward the outskirts of town, and I'm about to give him directions when he pulls off onto the street that leads to the back road for our trailer. Of course he knows where we live.

Gram is waiting outside when his car pulls up, her face drawn, and I try not to think about the last time she saw the sheriff pull up to her house.

"Thanks for bringing Sid home, Grant," she says as I hop out of the car, and he tips his hat at her like he's Andy Griffith. "Hope everything's all right."

"Everything's fine, Marybeth," he says, and I look between the two of them, because since when has Gram been on a first-name basis with Sheriff Kepler? Since when has she looked at him with anything but suspicion?

Gram leads me inside the trailer, one hand on my shoulder as the sheriff's car pulls away. I'm taller than she is, but right now, I don't feel like it.

"Sit," she says, and I take a seat at the kitchen table. After the silence of the sheriff's office I am itching to talk to her, to someone. Lilah Crenshaw is missing. Dad didn't do it but someone's doing this because of him—whether or not he's actually feeding someone information from inside prison, this is happening because of him, and I want to talk to her because she's the only person who will understand that. I want to ask her all the questions I could not ask five years ago.

Did you know what Dad was doing?

"What'd the sheriff want?" she asks as she puts a pan on the stove and fries up an egg for me.

"Another girl's gone missing."

"And?"

"And he wanted to know if I knew anything."

"Why would you know anything?" she asks.

"Because of Dad," I say, and I'm suddenly filled with a white-hot anger that I could not let myself feel earlier, of how unfair this all is. "The girl—Lilah and I were fighting on Thursday because she said I had something to do with—with all the girls going missing because of Dad and now she's gone missing and the sheriff thought that I—that I—"

I can't get the rest of the words out. I'm suddenly filled with this desperation to hug Gram, to cry into her shoulder like I haven't since I was thirteen.

"How could he even think that?" I choke out. I don't let myself cry, though. No matter how much my eyes burn, or how tight my throat feels. How much of a relief it would be.

I don't deserve relief.

"You know," Gram says, "before we moved out here, the few weeks I was still staying at your daddy's place with you, we got calls almost every day from people demanding to know why I hadn't done anything sooner." She sighs. "People went up there and did all sorts of shit when they found out where we lived. Harmless stuff, sometimes—toilet paper or eggs, mostly, though one time someone threw one of them Fourth of July sparklers in the pine straw. Nearly caught it on fire." She flips the egg before carefully sliding it onto a plate—the yolk still liquid, my favorite way to eat it.

I look down at the egg, think of the same sight splattered against the front of our house, back when we lived in a house. Try to picture it but can't.

"I think," she says after a minute, "you underestimate how much this town still hates what your daddy did, Sid. People've got good reason to be mad, especially with it happening again. And I think Grant Kepler feels like he has a lot to prove still, since he's the one who arrested your daddy the first time. Hell, there's probably people puttin' pressure on *him* to dig as deep as he can into us. That don't make it right, of course, and if he tries to take you in again I'll march down to that station myself and give him hell."

I take the last bite of my egg and push back from the table, and surprise us both when I go to hug Gram. The top of her head fits under my chin, and I breathe in her comforting scent, and I let her hold me, the only other person who understands what it's like to shoulder the burden of having my dad, her son, as part of our blood.

Gram does drive me to school the next day since my bike is still there. Her knuckles are white on the steering wheel. I hate that she has to do this, but I don't want to ask Sally Louise for a ride, even though she's my only other option besides Gram.

I could have asked Mavis, but I shove that thought away. She keeps reaching out to me, but I don't want to talk. I'm not ready.

The news vans are still parked in front of our school when she pulls up, and I hastily grab my backpack and hurry out of the car. It's not likely they'll recognize the car, but they might recognize Gram, and they might recognize me.

"Sid?" she asks as I shut the door. She rolls down the window and I duck my head back in.

"Yeah?"

"Don't make me do this again," she says, and I nod. I feel eyes on me, on us, and I turn. It's not a news anchor like I thought, but Mavis. When she sees me looking, she averts her gaze and walks inside.

"I'll see you at home. I'll call if I'm late."

"Be safe," she says, and I know she means it, but it doesn't make me feel protected like it did when I was younger.

"I will," I say, and my answer is equally hollow.

I pull my hood over my head as I walk up the path to school, trying to avoid catching the eye of the blond news anchor who's waiting by the fence. But I'm not quick enough and she makes eye contact with me, and for a second I think I see that spark of recognition in her features. I stiffen as she comes toward me, but she breezes right past me without a second look, and I turn.

It's Craig. Pulling into the parking lot in a beat-up Chevy that must be his sister's, like he thought that would fool them.

It doesn't. His windows are rolled up and he's driving as fast as he can for the parking lot, but the woman is jogging to keep up with his car, microphone in hand.

I don't even stop. Better Craig than me. He's got an alibi. The attention from the vultures will blow over for him soon, and he can be the carrion for once.

The news vans have left by the time school ends, which I'm grateful for, and Craig looks only slightly worse for wear.

I hop on my bike and begin to pedal hard, heading toward downtown. I've been thinking about what Sheriff Kepler said about the dates. About Lauren and June's insistence that I do something, that I try to solve this. Now that I know someone's copying the dates, I can figure out when the next one is.

Maybe if I'm lucky, I can figure out who might be next. And if I can solve this—

Then what?

Will I finally be free of him?

I chain my bike to the rack in front of the library, readjust my backpack. I know what I should be doing here. I should be catching up on homework that our teachers don't care about. I should be getting further ahead in *Jane Eyre*. But what's the point of reading the book when I can't bring myself to even talk to Mavis? She'd probably just end up doing all the work on whatever project we were assigned together, anyway.

I find a computer in the back corner of the library and log in, grateful Gram got me a library card when I was a kid because it was the one place she could bring me and I could just sit and read. The librarians never stared, or gossiped, or if they did they had the sense not to do it in front of us.

I used to like reading, as a kid. Back when I could pay attention to it, and fantasy books made it easy to escape everything happening, like the divorce.

They stopped working when Dad got arrested. There was no point anymore. Dragons and knights and girls who dressed as boys and went on quests, none of it mattered. It wouldn't bring him back, and it was just a reminder that I couldn't wave a wand or befriend a wise old wizard and have everything magically fixed.

The computer finally loads, probably one of the same ones I

used to play games on in middle school, since I don't think anything but the books have been updated here since then. We're not in a nice part of the county that might get funding.

I take a deep breath as I open a browser.

I know what I have to do, and it's not something I've ever wanted to—

I search for my dad's name. Not his victims, him. If someone really is copying Dad like I think, knowing as many details as possible about what he did is far more important than my own discomfort.

I'm immediately overwhelmed by the results, a whole Wikipedia page detailing his crimes. A subreddit for true-crime podcast fans discussing even more details. An entry on some site called Murderpedia with links to news articles about his arrest.

I feel sick. But I have to know. I can't stop scrolling. Several links to *Dawn of Justice* come up, the podcast Dawn Schaefer's family made, and I go ahead and download it on my phone to listen to later before pulling up another article.

Dennis Crane Gets Five Life Sentences

Thursday, October 9, 2014

Dennis Crane agreed to a guilty plea on Wednesday for the first-degree murders of Lauren O'Malley (18), Alicia Graves (19), Melissa Wagner (18), Dawn Schaefer (17), and Samantha Markham (17). Crane will serve five consecutive life sentences without the possibilty of parole. Dawn Schaefer's parents gave emotional victim impact statements in court.

"Frankly, I don't think this sentence is harsh enough," said Eddie Schaefer, who, along with wife, Kelly, and Bill and Rhonda Wagner, advocated that Crane receive the death penalty. "Our daughter is dead. He shouldn't get to rot away in prison on my tax dollars."

I exit out of the page, feeling sick. I can barely make it through one article; how am I going to get through the rest?

But I owe it to the girls to know. To remember.

October 9 was barely a month after my birthday. I knew, by then, that Dad wasn't coming back. He'd been indicted a few months before. I found out later that the death penalty had been advocated for, but the prosecutor was willing to go with five life sentences if he pled guilty. One for each life he took.

I pull up another article, one on Melissa's disappearance this time. It's not much, just a few paragraphs from the county paper.

Another Local Girl Missing

Cardinal Creek, North Carolina

Tuesday, January 29, 2008

Wayne County deputies are asking for the public's help in

locating missing eighteen-year-old Melissa Wagner, last seen January 26, 2008, near Holly Acres subdivision. It is unclear if her disappearance is connected with the murder of Lauren O'Malley and the disappearance of Alicia Graves two weeks ago. The public is asked to notify authorities of any information that could lead to finding Melissa.

January 26. January 26 as in Friday. The day Lilah went missing.

I click back and frantically search for Dawn Schaefer, Dad's fourth victim. I have to go back a page to find any information from her disappearance—all of the newer hits are articles about the Schaefers advocating for the death penalty or for the podcast. But finally I find the first article about her disappearance. It's dated March 1, 2008.

I have four weeks to figure out who's doing this before the fourth girl goes missing.

Melissa Wagner: January 26, 2008

MELISSA WAGNER'S sister ran a blog for a long time after her disappearance. She even wrote an article for the newspaper after my dad was sentenced, an opinion piece on if he should have gotten the death penalty like her parents and Dawn's parents were fighting for. Unlike them, she was against it, saying it wasn't what her sister would have wanted, that she didn't want to deprive anyone else of a family member the way she had been.

I don't think I could ever face her. I don't know what to say. Even if he's not dead, I haven't really had a father for years. Not in the way it counts.

A girl is driving her sister around to sell Girl Scout cookies. She's supposed to go with her up to the door, help her take orders, but she and Cassie quickly figured out that Cassie's got a lot more luck when her teenage sister isn't tagging along.

So a girl waits in the car for her little sister, and a man

approaches. She doesn't notice him at first. Why would she? This neighborhood is in a nicer part of town, plenty of people go jogging out here.

But he's not in jogging clothes, and by the time she realizes that, he's already almost at her car. It's too late to roll her window up. She'd rolled it down when Cassie got out of the car, mostly so she could smoke while Cassie was gone.

She's supposed to be keeping an eye on Cassie. It's only the first week of cookie season, and Cassie's a Brownie this year, determined to sell as many boxes of Girl Scout cookies as she can.

Melissa's a little proud of her, not that she'd admit that.

She flicks the ash from her cigarette onto the ground, just inches away from the man's tennis shoes. He looks at her with a grin. He's got sunglasses on, even though it's cloudy. All she sees is her own pissed-off reflection staring back at her.

"You're not supposed to be parked here," he says.

"You're not a cop." She doesn't know what makes her say it; her mother's raised her to be polite to strangers. But she's on edge, has been since Lauren and Alicia went missing.

Her mother almost didn't let them go out selling this year, but Cassie insisted. And her mother agreed, as long as Melissa would watch out for her.

"No, but I live here," he says. "You're blocking my driveway."

"No, you don't," she retorts. He frowns.

"And how do you know that?"

She jerks a thumb over her shoulder. "My sister's selling cookies in this neighborhood. I know what everyone looks like. You don't live here."

He gives her a sheepish grin, shrugs his shoulders. Something about it makes her uneasy. The grin feels fake.

"Caught me," he says. "I'm actually lost. This damn neighborhood's like a labyrinth." He gestures back to his car. "My wife gave me one of them GPS things, but I don't know how to work it." He leans a little, like he's looking in her car, and his face lights up. "You've got one! Think you could come help me out with mine?"

Melissa bites her lip. She wants to say no. She wants to roll up her window and drive off to the house Cassie's at and tell her they'll come back later.

But her parents have always told her to be polite, to be helpful, and Cassie'll pitch a fit if they have to leave now.

"Sure," she says, and gets out of the car. She follows him to his—it's an old beige Buick, not unlike her dad's. He opens the passenger door for her.

"It's on the dash. If you'd just program it for me that'd be great."

"Sure," she says again. "What address?"

He doesn't answer her. She turns, thinking maybe he didn't hear her, but before she fully can, there's a rag clamped over her mouth, her vision blurring, something sharp and chemical in her nose.

When her sister comes back to the car, there's no sign of Melissa, or the man. She knocks on the neighbors' doors, but no one saw anything.

She calls her mother to come pick her up with the cell phone in the car that's for emergencies only.

She quits Girl Scouts the next year.

Chapter Eight

I BARELY say hello to Gram when I get home. If she asks about the funeral, I don't hear her. My mind is too busy.

"I have homework," I call, just before I shut my door and sit down at my desk.

I put in my earbuds and queue up *Dawn of Justice*, though I hesitate right before I click play. Reading articles was one thing. Listening to the family members of one of Dad's victims?

It feels worse than the ghosts, even if it's becoming harder and harder to convince myself they're not real—like with June grabbing my hoodie. Actually hearing their family talk about what Dad did, about how it impacted them—am I ready for that?

I have to be. Something tells me if I'm not, the girls will show up and force me to listen, anyway. I owe this to them.

My finger hovers over the play button on the podcast. What am I listening for, exactly? Clues? Something that might help me?

I pull out my notes from the library and stare down at them. Why did my dad pick Dawn? Why was there almost a month in between her death and the other girls?

Was he trying to stop killing? Or was he almost caught?

I push play. The audio quality isn't great, like it was recorded in someone's garage or something.

"Hi. My name is Jeremy Schaefer. In 2008, my sister, Dawn, was murdered by serial killer Dennis Crane. I'm going to take you through what we know of the last days of her life, because she deserves to be remembered alive. Nothing here for y'all true-crime junkies or fucking rubberneckers trying to get off on my family's tragedy. I'm doing this because y'all need to know what happened to my sister, so you'll agree with me when I say that Dennis Crane deserves the death penalty, and we will be fighting like hell to make sure he gets it."

I check the release date of the episode—July 13, 2014. Over six years after Dawn's murder. Only a few months before my dad was sentenced.

I know Jeremy and his family weren't successful in advocating for the death penalty, but a shiver runs down my spine all the same at his words. I can feel his anger, his family's anger, even through my shitty earbuds.

Worse? I can't blame them for it. I didn't know until today that that had even been on the table. It's not like I was there when he was sentenced; I was too young. Some of the families didn't think the life sentences were enough, and I don't know that I could argue with them if given the chance. He killed their daughters.

I make myself keep listening.

"My sister went missing on February 28, 2008. I was supposed to pick her up from school that day. She stayed late because she had rehearsal for the school musical. Now, here's something you have to understand about me and my sister—I hate musicals. And I hated picking her up from school. I was nineteen. I had other shit to do. So I didn't want to go get her, kept dragging my feet. Ended up there thirty minutes late." There's the sound of a shaky breath, and then the guy continues. "I will never forgive myself for those thirty minutes."

There's a crackling in the audio and then the quality changes, music coming through, distorted by static. It's a song I vaguely recognize, though I'm not sure why until someone starts singing.

Oh god. It's "Somewhere Over the Rainbow." From *The Wizard of Oz*. I used to watch that movie as a kid over and over. It's one of Gram's favorites.

It's one of Dad's favorites, too.

Whoever's singing the song has a good voice, low and strong even with the terrible audio quality, and I close my eyes, absorbed in it. The song ends too quickly, before the last verse is even over. Jeremy's voice cuts back in.

"That was my sister. That's the last recording I have of her. Some girl in the cast took it during rehearsal and sent it to me after she died. The last recording I have of her voice." His own voice breaks, and he starts sobbing. I yank my earbuds out of my ears.

I don't know if I can hear more of this. The rawness of Jeremy's voice, his grief on display. Dawn's voice. Jeremy will never get to hear his sister sing that song again and it is because of my father and I don't know how I feel about that. If I'm even allowed to feel anything about that.

No. I have to feel something about it. If I don't feel anything about their deaths, I'll be just like my dad. I have to feel *something.*

I pick my earbuds back up and put them in my ears, and press play again.

"I waited in my car for fifteen minutes before I realized Dawn wasn't coming out of the school," Jeremy says, his voice still scratchy. "She didn't have a phone. I'd only just gotten one the month before, so I had no way to reach her. I'm telling you this so you understand—I *tried*. I went in and asked around for her, but no one had seen her and by then she was gone. No one had seen her leave. The details came out later. Dawn accepted a ride from the man we now know is Dennis Crane, who worked at the post office on Guilford Street before it was closed and remodeled. She accepted a ride from him sometime between five and five-thirty, and he immediately drove her out to Cardinal Lake, where he strangled her, shaved her head, and dumped her body." Jeremy's voice grows louder. “The cops said it only took him about twenty minutes, and then he went home to his kid.”

I’m going to be sick. I can’t listen to this. I can’t hear the rest of it, the details of what my father did to Dawn, Melissa, Samantha, Alicia, Lauren.

But I can’t stop listening. I’m frozen in place, like someone is pinning me to my chair.

There are hands on my ankles. There is lake water in my lungs.

“Now,” Dawn whispers in my ear in that low voice, “you know how it feels.”

I give myself half an hour to recover. Half an hour to pull myself back together before I listen to the rest of the episodes. There are only three, like maybe Jeremy didn’t want to finish it, or maybe it was always supposed to be this length.

I look back down at my notes before I start again—a list of all of my dad’s victims with the dates they went missing and the dates they were found.

LAUREN O’MALLEY–JANUARY 8, 2008
FOUND: JANUARY 27, 2008
ALICIA GRAVES–JANUARY 16, 2008
FOUND: FEBRUARY 3, 2008
MELISSA WAGNER–JANUARY 26, 2008
FOUND: JANUARY 30, 2008

DAWN SCHAEFER–FEBRUARY 28, 2008
FOUND: MARCH 3, 2008
SAMANTHA MARKHAM–MARCH 4, 2008
FOUND: MARCH 11, 2008

I stare down at all of them. There's a month between Melissa and Dawn—why? I know from what I found at the library that when Lauren went missing, the police hadn't known they were dealing with a serial killer. Same with Melissa. It wasn't until Alicia, the third girl found, that they had any idea.

Is that why he stopped between them? Were the police on to him? Nothing I've found from old articles suggests that, so he could have just been paranoid—or if he was working with someone, maybe they killed the final two girls. Not Dad.

I hit play, my pen poised over the notebook, ready to add any new information from the rest of the podcast.

But the more I listen, the more I realize—this isn't an investigation. It's a memorial. There are interviews with some of Dawn's high school friends, with some of my teachers even. The last episode is entirely devoted to talking about what Dawn was like as a child, so that when it finishes, I feel like *I* almost knew her.

"But you didn't."

I whip around. It's not Dawn. It's Savannah. She's in the same clothes she was in the day she went missing. I recognize them from her sitting near me in class. Like June, she's half rotting. Unlike June, only half of her hair is shaved. She runs her fingers through what remains, laughing softly. It echoes.

"Guess he didn't finish the job," she says. She cocks her head and looks at me. "That wouldn't be a problem with you."

My fists clench. "I'm not a target."

"Are you sure?" she asks.

"My dad wouldn't—he wouldn't kill me—"

"Wake *up*, Sid," she says, and then she's leaning in, her hands on my shoulders. "This isn't about him anymore. Do you seriously believe all this bullshit about him having an accomplice and *maybe someone helped him*? I think you need to stop worrying so much about *if* he's got help now and start worrying about the fact that someone is doing this *because of him*."

She laughs, and it's high and cold.

"And if someone's doing this because of him, who do you think they're going to target, hmm? Which girl is going to be the fifth one?"

"I'm not a girl." It comes out automatically, a reflex. "You—you wouldn't know that, though. You're not real."

"I'm not?" She caresses my cheek, and I shiver. "If I weren't real I think I *would* know that, Sid. If I were just some product of your imagination, I'd know *everything about you*."

"Why don't you leave me alone?" I beg. "Or why don't you . . . haunt the sheriff or the coroner or something—"

"They wouldn't see me, Sid. No one sees me but you. No one sees *us* but you."

Her hands wrap around my throat, and for a terrifying moment I think she's going to kill me, that I'm going to feel what she did in her last moments of life, but then Gram knocks on the door.

"Sid? Phone call."

Savannah vanishes, and I'm left trying desperately not to gasp for breath as Gram opens the door. I scramble to shut my notebook and flip my phone over so Gram can't see the screen—not that I think she'd recognize the podcast, but still. I don't need her to know how deep I'm getting into this.

"Who is it?" I ask as she holds the phone out to me. She frowns at me.

"Your father," she says, like it's obvious, and then I realize it should be. She's holding the landline, and he tries to call every few weeks.

"Did you accept the call already?" I ask, and she nods. I take the phone from her, cradle it to my ear as she leaves.

"Dad?" My voice shakes, and I hope he doesn't notice.

"Sid," he says. "How're you holding up?"

I'm surprised at the question. Dad rarely asks about how I am unless it's some perfunctory thing about school. I used to think it was because he didn't care, but now I think it's for a different reason. Maybe he really doesn't want to know. We both know how fucked-up I am because of what he did. Why should I have to remind him?

"Fine," I say, but I can't help glancing around my room for

Savannah, wondering if she'll come back now, while I'm talking to him. Her or June. My shoulders tense. I pick up my pen and open my notebook, just to give myself something to do.

My eyes land on the dates again. "Another girl's missing," I blurt out.

"I know," he says. "We get the news up here, too."

"Right," I say. Right. Of course he knows. Of course he would know. I find myself analyzing the tone of his voice—was he too casual when he said that? Too obvious? Is there anything there that would tell me if he's responsible for what's going on right now?

Savannah's voice creeps back into my head. *Who do you think they're going to target, hmm?*

He would know. If someone was going to target me—even if he didn't know who. He would know better than anyone how a killer thinks.

I'm not going to be able to ask him about that now, not on a fifteen-minute phone call.

"Dad? Can I . . . can I come visit?"

There's silence on the other end of the line, stretching out so long I think he's hung up. "Dad?"

"Why would you want to do that?" he finally asks. It cuts more than anything else he's said in a while. I can't just say, "Because you're my dad." That's not how this works. That's not how our relationship goes.

"Because I need to talk to you about what's happening," I

say. *Because I'm worried I might be a target. Because I need to know you don't have a hand in this. Because what if you do and you want me dead?* "I don't want to do it over the phone."

I wait. For a second I think he'll say no. I've only visited him a handful of times when I was younger, and I haven't been in almost a year. But I need this. I need to talk to him.

"Sure, Sid," he finally says. "When?"

"This weekend," I say. "Does that . . . does that work?" *Another girl won't go missing for a while,* I tell myself. I have time.

Lilah Crenshaw doesn't, but I can't let myself think about that.

"Yeah," he says. "I'm sure it does. You're approved and everything, and you're old enough Marybeth won't need to come with you."

Gram became Marybeth after Dad was arrested. Not Mom. Not Gram.

"Okay," I say. "I'll see you then. Do you . . . do you need money, or anything, I can ask Gram—"

"No," he says instantly. "I'm fine up here. The Jell-O won't kill me."

"You're sure?" I ask, because it's our thing. It's something we share, but he doesn't laugh. Instead I hear the click of the line that tells me he's hung up.

He doesn't tell me he loves me. He hasn't since the day he was sentenced.

I can't even tell if I miss it or not. Or if I only miss what could have been, if he hadn't fucked everything up.

If he hadn't killed the girls.

It doesn't really hit me until the next day that in order to go see Dad, to go talk to him, I need a ride. Gram won't drive on the highway anymore, hasn't for the past year. And I can't drive myself.

Maybe I should've taken Mavis up on her offer to teach me how to drive. But I certainly can't ask her about it now.

Really, there's only one other person I can ask.

I go look for Sally at lunch, knowing that unlike me she usually eats in the lunchroom. Normally she eats with Lilah, but Lilah isn't here.

I'm about to head down the hall to the lunchroom when a woman brushes past me, her elbow nearly colliding with my stomach. I skirt out of her way in time, and turn, thinking it's a teacher, or staff.

It isn't. She turns, too, and suddenly I'm face-to-face with Lilah Crenshaw's mother.

"Sorry," I say, even though she's the one who collided with me. She frowns, her eyes narrowing. They're the exact same shape as Lilah's.

She knows who I am. She has the same expression she did the day she saw me at the search, but up close, it pierces even more.

I want to tell her. I want to say that I have nothing to do with her daughter's disappearance, that I need her to know that, to understand. That her daughter and I may not have gotten along much, but I'd never . . . I wouldn't kill her. I want to say it just so she'll stop looking at me the way she is right now.

But it wouldn't matter. It's not me she sees when she looks at me, not really. It's my dad.

"Mrs. Crenshaw," I begin, but she holds up a hand.

"My daughter is missing," she says, her voice tight. "So unless you're about to tell me you know where she is, I don't want to hear anything you have to say."

She walks away before I can even react, and then June wraps her icy fingers around my throat, leans in to whisper in my ear.

"You are never," she says, "going to escape what he's done."

I don't have it in me to not believe her.

I decide to wait until third period to talk to Sally Louise. I know she has study hall, since I tried to get that as a class too and was denied because it was apparently "already full." Like a study hall can be full.

But study hall means there will be fewer people around to see us talk, which is what I'm hoping for. I wait until five minutes after the last lunch bell rings before heading inside. I can be late to civics; it's not like we're doing anything interesting, anyway.

I find Sally Louise in a back corner, her head bent over our calculus textbook. Somehow she knows it's me without even looking.

"What do you want, Sid?"

She finally glances up, and I flinch. She looks like a mess. I've never seen her not put together, but even though her hair is in a ponytail, it doesn't disguise that it hasn't been washed in a day or two. She's not wearing makeup either, which isn't normal for Sally Louise.

For a second, I think, *I shouldn't be here. I shouldn't be doing this.* I should be offering to help her, not asking her for another favor.

But the best way I can help is by figuring out who's killing the girls and stopping it altogether.

"I need your help," I say. She frowns, but I continue. "I need—I need you to drive me to the prison on Saturday. I have to talk to my dad. I can't ask the sheriff for any more information and I need to find out what's happening. Dad will have information. He'll know how this guy thinks and I can't . . . I don't have anyone else to ask. Please."

Sally Louise sighs. "I don't know, Sid."

"You already helped me once. You know I didn't have anything to do with it," I say. "And it could help us find Lilah."

"Don't bring Lilah into it," Sally Louise snaps. "Don't pretend like you care about finding her."

"I do," I say. "Please, I know I didn't get along with her,

but that doesn't mean I want—"

She cuts me off. "Do you really think your dad will be able to tell you anything helpful?"

"Yes," I say. "I do. If someone's copying him, then—"

Sally nods. She doesn't contradict me. She knows someone probably is copying Dad, and the more information we can get, the better.

"Okay," she says, and I look at her.

"What?"

"I said okay. I'll drive you to the prison. But you owe me *big*-time, Atkinson," she says, and the knot of fear unfurls just a little in my chest, because she used my name. Mine. Not my dad's.

"I'll buy you a burger or something on the way back."

"Make it a Cook Out milkshake and I'll *maybe* consider us even," she says. "Now can you leave me alone? I actually want to pass this semester, even if you don't."

She puts her head back down, but as I leave I turn back and glance at her. She's almost, almost smiling.

Almost.

There are news vans in the parking lot as I'm leaving, a reporter with a microphone standing by the sign for our school. I pull my hood over my head and unlock my bike, so focused on undoing the chain that I don't realize the reporter is standing near me until it's too late.

"Hi there," she says as I turn around. "Are you a student here?"

"Yes," I say, resisting the urge to retort *obviously*, knowing that anything I say can be taken, twisted out of context. She beams.

"Great! Would you mind answering a few questions about the disappearances that have been happening around Cardinal Creek High?"

I look at her. Really look at her. She's white, with ginger hair that doesn't look like a dye job, pink-toned skin, and foundation caked on that's covering what I'm sure are freckles. She looks only a few years older than me, too young to have been working when my dad was arrested.

But if this airs, that won't matter. Anyone in this town who watches it knows who I am.

"I need to get home," I say, as sweetly and apologetically as I can. But the lock on my bike sticks, enough that I'm still stuck there while she's holding a microphone in my face. When I finally do get free, the reporter doesn't let me pass.

"It'll take two minutes," she says. "We just want a teen's perspective. Especially a girl's perspective. What's your name?"

She's not going to let me get out of this. And while it would be tempting to be rude, her camera's still on.

"Sidney Atkinson," I say. She doesn't react to my name, but I don't drop my guard.

"Sidney, great," she says, smiling wide. "Now. Were you

close with any of the missing girls?"

"No," I say automatically.

"How do you feel, knowing that someone is out there, stalking girls like you?"

I bristle at this but let it go. I have to be polite. "It's . . . it's terrifying, I guess." I shift my weight from foot to foot. I want to be anywhere else but here. I've spent so long avoiding this, dreading it, that I haven't actually thought of what I'd say to get out of it.

"Great. Now. I know you might've been too young, but are you familiar at all with the serial murders that happened in Cardinal Lake ten years ago?"

"I . . ." My mouth is dry. I can't answer. After a minute the reporter realizes that, and she looks at me.

And that's when I see it. That recognition.

"What did you say your name was?" she asks slowly.

"Sidney. Atkinson," I add.

"Sidney."

I hate the way she says my name.

"I know you, don't I, Sidney?"

"No," I say. "I don't think you do."

"I do," she insists, and then she's leaning in, studying me like I'm a specimen from our biology class, or some piece of art she hasn't figured out yet if she likes or not. "I definitely do. Brady, where do I know her from?"

It's only then that I notice the cameraman. I flinch away

from the light on the camera that indicates he's filming.

"She looks like him," he says, and there's no question which *him* he's referring to. "Don't she?"

"That's gotta be it," the woman says, and turns back to me. "I know you."

"No, you don't," I say more firmly, already ready to bolt, to leave, when someone loops my arm through theirs.

"I didn't think you were allowed to be on school property," Mavis's voice says. "Since we're minors and all."

"That's only during school hours, dear," the woman says, but Mavis gives her a glare that stops her from continuing. "I think we have all we need from your friend here, anyway." She gives Mavis the same dazzling smile she gave me.

"Did my friend consent to being interviewed by you?" Mavis asks coldly. "Or did you just come up and start asking invasive questions?"

The woman flushes. "I—"

"I think you should leave," Mavis says. "And if I were you I'd think twice about airing an interview I didn't obtain legally."

The woman sputters, but she and the cameraman leave, and I let out a small sigh of relief, my heart still racing.

"Fucking vultures," Mavis spits, and then disentangles her arm from mine. I'm still shaking from the adrenaline, so much that I don't even realize she's gone until I look up and she's half-way across the parking lot.

"Mavis, wait," I say, starting to jog after her—as much as I can with my bike. "I . . . I want to talk to you."

She turns around. "Oh, you're finally talking to me again, Sid?"

I flinch, thinking of the voice mails she's left, the unread texts on my phone. "I just . . . wanted to thank you."

"Don't mention it," she says. There's tension still in the lines of her body, but after a minute, she relaxes slightly.

I *miss* her.

"Mavis . . ."

"I have to go, Sid," she says, and even though I want to apologize, even though I have so much I still need to say to her, I let her go before I can.

Lilah Crenshaw: January 26, 2018

A GIRL'S mother berates her as soon as she walks in the door.

"You missed church," she says. *"Again.* We could've used your help today."

The girl sighs, sets her backpack down. She knew this lecture was coming, has known it since she skipped youth group Wednesday and prep for the food drive tonight.

"I was at Sally's, remember?" she says. "We were studying."

At the mention of Sally, her mother softens. Sally Louise is the Right Kind of Girl for Lilah to be hanging out with, even if she does cause her to miss church every once in a while.

Lilah wasn't at Sally's, of course. She was at her boyfriend's, who her mother absolutely doesn't approve of. She especially wouldn't approve if she knew what they were up to. It's not the kind of thing good Christian girls do, getting high on weekends, but it keeps her from thinking about the stress of everything else.

Thinking about that stress causes panic to rise up in her throat, but she stuffs it down. If her mother sees her panic, she'll send her back to the doctor for another round of talking and meds, and she doesn't know how to make it clear that the actual panic isn't the problem, it's her mother. Her mother and her expectations.

She can't be in this house a moment longer.

"I'm going for a drive," she says, and heads out the door before her mother can respond, knowing she's going to get hell for it later and not really caring.

She drives around until it gets dark, until the gas light in her car comes on. She thought about just driving back to her boyfriend's, but she realized when she got in the car that all she wanted to be was *alone*. No expectations of who she's supposed to be. The devoted girlfriend, the ambitious daughter. Only Sally really gets that, and she doesn't even talk to her about it that much.

She stops at a stoplight on Main Street, one that stays red forever. She's behind a pickup truck, and she catches a glimpse of a man's face in the side mirror. Something about it chills her, but she doesn't know what.

The light changes, and they both drive down Main Street before he slows his car to a crawl, pulling it off to the side. She goes around him, more annoyed now than panicked, but he pulls his car out just as quickly, nearly riding her bumper.

She thinks of Savannah. She thinks of June. She picks up the pace, going way over the speed limit, hoping some of Sheriff Kepler's boys aren't out patrolling tonight, because they'll surely call her mother.

Abruptly she turns down a side road, one she knows no one goes down, just to confirm what she's thinking. To her horror, the truck turns, too, and now she knows he's following her.

The truck flashes its headlights at her. She speeds up, and it does, too. She feels the impact when it taps her car, the sound louder than she ever would have thought, and she swerves off the road into a ditch.

"Shit," she breathes. "Shit shit shit." She puts the car in park, fumbles around for her phone until she remembers she tossed it in the back seat so she wouldn't be distracted by her mother calling.

She unbuckles, crawling over her seat to reach her phone, but in the chaos it's slid where she can't reach.

She's going to have to get out of the car.

"Just drive away," she tells herself, but she knows she can't. The truck is still parked behind her; she can see its headlights reflecting off her mirrors, and she knows whoever this asshole is he'll probably follow her home, and she doesn't want him to know where she lives.

"Fuck," she hisses and wrenches open her driver's side door, launching herself out of the car.

But it's too late. An arm wraps around her chest and she wants to kick or scream or bite but then panic engulfs her and she forgets how to even breathe.

Chapter Nine

GRAM TEXTS as I'm just leaving the parking lot, asking if I can stop at the gas station on the way home to pick up a few things, says she'll pay me back. I stuff my phone in my sweatshirt pocket and hurry to the gas station, hoping I can get there and home before dark. I normally wouldn't worry, but Gram insisted, and after what happened with the reporter just now I'm jumpy enough to take her advice.

The parking lot is more full than it normally is when I'm there at night, and my stomach turns at the sight. I want to go home. I don't want to be here.

But Gram told me to pick up things, and I'm not going to disappoint her. If I get in and out quickly, it'll be fine.

I park my bike and head inside the QuikMart. There are at least five people in here, not counting Terry behind the counter. I have to squeeze past a man looking at bags of chips, keeping my head down and hood up. I head to the back and grab a few cans of soup and some pork rinds, and make my way to the fridge to get a Pepsi for Gram.

There's a white woman already there, her hair pulled back in a ponytail. When she sees me she steps aside, and I pretend not to notice as she does a double take. I've had enough of this today.

I take my stuff up to the counter. The woman is in line behind me now, standing far too close. Terry rings me up, but something's off. He doesn't say a word. There's a small TV behind him, turned to a local station, and his eyes keep darting to it rather than to me.

The woman behind me huffs, and I take my bag of stuff before remembering I also want a pack of cigarettes.

"Um. Morleys, too. Sorry," I say, and I hear her sigh, tap her foot. Without a word Terry grabs the pack, and I pull out my wallet, dig around in it for change. I manage to scrounge up enough and hand it to him, putting any extra in the Folgers coffee can for Lilah. Not that it'll matter, not that it'll make a difference.

"Unbelievable," the woman mutters, and this time I do whip around. She's scowling at me, at the can.

And then I hear a voice. My voice, and I turn, because for one moment I think I've finally snapped, that I've become a ghost myself.

But no. It's just me, on the TV, that interview with the reporter. She did air it.

I run out of the gas station before I have to see or hear anything else, realizing only when I'm halfway on my bike that I forgot my cigarettes; that they're just lying on the counter next to a photo of Lilah Crenshaw, begging for someone to see her.

Someone who isn't me.

I pedal as hard as I can for the first mile home, wanting to put some distance between myself and the gas station. I take back roads so I don't have to see the billboard.

I'm about two miles from home, riding half on the shoulder, when I hear a truck behind me. I slow, wait for it to pass, but it doesn't. If anything it slows down, matching my speed.

What the fuck?

I coast back onto the road, and then all of a sudden it speeds up, and I swerve just as it barrels past me, nearly hitting me with the side mirror. I scream, knowing I'm going to fall, bracing for the impact as I go down and roll into a ditch. The bag of food goes flying, the cans rolling off somewhere I can't see them.

Shit. Shit, just what I need to top off the rest of today. I lay my bike down and go to pick up the rest of the cans, the Pepsi, collecting them all back in the torn plastic bag. My wrist hurts, but not enough to stop me right now.

I make my way back to my bike, and it's only then I notice that the truck has stopped, like it's waiting for me.

I start toward the truck, not even really cognizant that I'm doing so until I'm almost on it. It looks familiar, and I realize I saw it earlier today, in the parking lot at the gas station.

The windows are so tinted I can't see the driver.

"Hey!" I shout, my voice hoarse. I stumble toward the truck, but just as I'm about to reach it it speeds off, and I lurch backward, stumbling into the ditch again.

My heart is pounding in my chest. Was it Terry? Johnny? I don't think they could have left the gas station that fast, but maybe—

Was it whoever is killing the girls?

Am I next? Or was someone just trying to fuck with me?

"Might wanna figure that out, babe," June says, and for once, I listen to her, finally pulling myself together and heading home.

It takes me longer than usual to get home—the bike's got a flat tire and the seat is twisted, so I had to walk it the rest of the way. Gram has the news on when I come in. I can only hope she missed seeing me on it.

"You're safe," she says, and to my surprise comes over and hugs me. The bag of stuff jostles against my hip as she does. "You all right? You're covered in dirt."

"Fell off the bike," I say. I don't mention the truck. No use worrying her further.

"I'm gonna shower," I say, and she goes back to her chair. "And you're gonna want to wait to open that Pepsi; it got a little shook up when I fell."

"As long as you didn't crush my pork rinds," she says, and I laugh, wincing as I do at the pain in my ribs.

I take a shower and then change, eating some leftover boxed mac and cheese before heading outside to see if I can do any sort of repair to my bike. I use the flashlight on my phone to look at it. Every snap of a twig, every rustle of a leaf, makes me jump.

I realize quickly that the hole on my bike wheel is too big to patch myself, and I swear. I'm going to need a ride to school tomorrow, and after what happened today with the reporters, I'm not asking Gram. If they recognized me, they'll certainly recognize her. I've already asked too many favors of Sally Louise.

My phone buzzes, and this time I do look down at it.

Just saw the news. You okay???

Mavis. I've been ignoring her texts, but she helped me today, and she's checking in now and I . . . I miss her. I miss the one person who doesn't look at me the way everyone else around here does, who actually *gets* me.

Maybe I've shut her out long enough.

I head inside and send her a text before I chicken out.

Fine I guess. Thanks again for today . . . also I might need a ride tomorrow. Bike's busted.

I tap my fingers impatiently against my leg while I wait for her to reply. Gram's asleep, but the TV's still running. She had it on *Jeopardy!* for once, but I hear the familiar intro to the nightly news.

My phone buzzes almost a second later with a text from Mavis.

Sure. I'll pick you up. Just send me your address.

Address. Shit. She's going to see where I live.

But I guess I have no choice. Beggars with broken bikes can't be choosers.

I send it to her and see that she's seen it. She doesn't respond again, and I know that's all I'm going to get from her tonight. I can properly apologize tomorrow. It doesn't feel right to do it over text.

I go get ready for bed, brush my teeth, and change into pj's. As I'm in the bathroom I hear a familiar voice over the TV screen for the second time today, though thank god this time it isn't my own.

I go back into the living room. Gram's still asleep, but there on the screen is Sheriff Kepler, Savannah's yearbook photo from last year in a tiny corner of the screen under his face.

I know what that means. Her body's finally been found.

"Good guess," she whispers in my ear, and it takes everything in me not to scream.

I'm already outside when Mavis pulls up the next morning; I don't want Gram to ask any more questions. When she'd asked how I was getting to school, I'd told her it was a friend, and when she'd asked if it was Sally and I'd said no, she'd just smirked a little.

"If your friend can drop you off after school, that'd be nice," she'd said, and I'd run out the door before I had to endure any more.

Mavis gets out of the car just as I'm almost at the passenger side, and I watch as she takes in our trailer, the remote isolation of it, the size. But she doesn't say anything about it like I thought she would. Instead, she goes to look at my bike.

"Damn, you really fucked it up," she says, looking at the tire. I managed to at least get the seat facing the right way again. "What happened?"

"Tell you in the car," I say. But to my surprise, Mavis grabs my bike and heads toward her trunk.

"My dad can fix it tonight," she says. "I'll get it back to you tomorrow."

"You don't have to do that—"

"It's for both of us. I can't drive you every day."

I'm about to protest more, but then I see Gram's silhouette approaching the front door, and that's the last thing I want right now. "Let's go."

We drive down the back road that leads away from the trailer. Mavis's car is clean, and warm, and she's got her phone plugged in playing some quiet jazz music.

"Thanks again for driving me," I say. "I really should learn how."

"I said I'd teach you," she says. A faint smile plays at the corners of her mouth.

"I didn't think—"

"Didn't think I'd still want to?" she asks. "Didn't think I'd want to spend time with you or get to know you once I found out who your dad was?"

"Yes," I say quietly. I clench my fists in my lap. Without taking her eyes off the road, Mavis reaches over, her hand covering mine, forcing it to relax.

"I can decide that for myself, Sid," she says. "You should have let me decide that for myself."

"I'm sorry," I say. "I just . . . everyone else down here *knows* and they'll never let me forget who I am, and just once I thought—I wanted that. I wanted you to like me, to want to get to know me, without any sort of idea of who my dad is or who you thought I was because of him." I swallow, and tentatively grip her hand back. "I'm sorry," I say again.

"I forgive you," she says. "I am serious about teaching you how to drive, if you want. I've got time after school."

"Yeah?"

"Yeah," she says. "What happened to your bike, anyway?"

"It's a long story," I say. I know I'm putting it off again, and I want to tell her, but it feels too big for right now and I know she'll start to worry. "Can we talk about something else?"

"As long as you're going to talk," she says, and I glare at her. "Sorry," she says, but she's smiling. "I couldn't resist."

I shake my head, but if she's bantering with me, we could almost be back to normal, no ghosts or regrets between us.

"Are we . . . are we good?" I ask, because I have to ask,

because I need that confirmation.

"Yeah, Sid," she says after a minute, just as we pull into the parking lot. "We're good."

"You sure?"

"Only if you've actually done the reading for *Jane Eyre*," she deadpans, and this time I do let myself laugh.

"Hey, I had to do something while I wasn't talking to you," I say. She laughs and squeezes my hand again.

I don't want her to let go.

Mavis is waiting for me in the parking lot after school. The atmosphere was hushed today, news of Savannah's death and Lilah's continued disappearance putting a damper on everything, rumors included. At this rate any of us will be lucky if we get through the year with our grades intact. I'm surprised they don't just shut everything down, but to this town that would be admitting defeat.

We wait until the parking lot clears, sitting in Mavis's car with the windows rolled up and the heat on. Our backpacks are by my feet, and I can see the corner of her sketchpad peeking out of hers.

"How's that going?" I ask, indicating it.

"Hmm?"

"The drawing," I say. "Or art class. I don't really know how that works."

"Oh," Mavis says. She gives a small laugh. "It's AP Art, so I have to pick a subject and do a final series of drawings."

"What's your subject?"

"Grief," she says, but she doesn't elaborate. She leans her head against the headrest, closes her eyes. "What really happened to your bike, Sid?"

I'm so startled by the change of subject that I don't answer her immediately.

"I crashed," I finally say. "Because someone ran me off the road. On purpose."

I tell her the rest. I tell her about the gas station, the truck nearly clipping me with its mirror. I don't tell her the horrible thought that's entered my mind because of it—

What if I'm next? Someone's copying Dad—the method, the dates. I have to assume they're copying the number of girls, too.

LAUREN O'MALLEY
ALICIA GRAVES
MELISSA WAGNER
DAWN SCHAEFER
SAMANTHA MARKHAM

I can't shake the feeling I won't be the next one, though I don't know why I feel so certain about that. But if this is someone's idea of revenge against Dad, leaving me for last would make the most sense.

If I'm last, though, I have to figure out who's next. And if the killer really is copying Dad's dates, I have a little under four weeks to figure it out. Dawn Schaefer went missing at the end of February. If I can figure out who's doing this by then, I can stop him before another girl gets killed.

God, that doesn't even begin to narrow down any suspects, though. I'd have to look at the whole fucking town.

I try not to think about Lilah. Don't want to admit to myself that it might be too late for her.

"I think you need to be careful, Sid," Mavis says, and when she looks at me again there's real worry in her eyes. "Getting involved in this isn't the best idea."

"I'm already involved in it," I say, frustrated. "I got *involved in it* when Dad—"

I can't finish that sentence, though. I know what the look on Mavis's face will be if I do.

Pity.

"You don't have to help," I tell her. "You don't—I'm not asking you to be involved in any of it. It's enough that I have to live with it. But I have to do something, Mavis. I have to figure out what's happening to these girls."

Mavis draws in a shuddery breath, then to my absolute bewilderment, starts crying.

I don't know what to do. I stare at her. I can barely deal with my own grief; someone else's is another thing entirely.

"Mavis, I—shit, I'm sorry, I didn't know you'd . . . I'm not going to die, I promise, but I can't just do *nothing*—"

"It's not that," she sniffs, and hiccups. "That came out wrong. Obviously I don't want you to die. But it's not that, Sid, it's . . ." She sniffs again, leans over me, and opens her console and pulls out a napkin, wiping her eyes with it.

"I have to tell you something," she says, her voice raw. "About why we moved here." She takes another deep breath, as if steeling herself. "We moved here because my sister . . . my sister was murdered," she says quietly.

It's the last thing I'm expecting. All her cryptic comments, all the things she said when we first met—this isn't what I expected at all.

"What?"

"My sister," she gasps, then wipes at her eyes with the heel of her hand. "My little sister, Ginny, went missing four years ago. She was seven. They don't . . . they haven't found her. Never found who did it. And this fall is coming up on five years and I know they're not going to find her, because she's *dead*, it's been so long that she has to be dead, but my mom didn't want to give up hope and wanted to reopen the search, but then Dad got this job offer and—and we're here." She laughs. "Dad knew about the murders when we moved, of course, but I think in his mind that means it wouldn't happen again. Lightning striking and all that. That first day when everyone was staring at me, I thought it was because they knew about Ginny. But it wasn't. It was because of June. And because of *you*."

"Mavis, I . . ."

Mavis shakes her head, too quick. "Mom and Dad don't see me. Not since Ginny went missing. They still think she's out there, but I know she's not. And they keep wanting to dig it up, when I spent my childhood answering questions from nosy reporters about my sister. Like that would help anyone find her." Her voice is raw with grief. "I miss her *so much*, and then when we moved here and all this started again, I thought . . . God, what if it's me? What if I'm just—just fucking *cursed*?" She laughs. "It was almost a relief when I found out who you were. Because at least this time, it wasn't my fault, that all of this was happening."

It is my turn to draw in a breath, to try to close my eyes against this. When I open them again, Mavis is looking directly at me.

"My sister is dead because of someone like your dad, Sid," she says quietly. There's no accusation in her tone, but I feel it all the same. "So I'm sorry, but I can't help you with this. I've done enough investigating on my own about Ginny. I can't go through it again."

"I understand," I say. "And I'm sorry."

"I'm not going to tell you not to do it, but . . . please, please be careful. You don't know—" She stops herself before she finishes the sentence. I know what it was, though.

You don't know what you're up against.

That's the problem, though.

I do.

We switch sides in the car after a few minutes, once we've both calmed down enough for Mavis to actually teach me how to drive. She's good, patient. I keep catching her eye and then looking away.

I understand her more, now. Why she left the search for Savannah, why she's been cagey if I've asked about her family.

It's such a relief to finally be talking with her again. Even if I can't talk about Dad. At least she knows; at least I'm not hiding it from her. She's been through it, just in a different way.

Driving, at least, turns out to be easier than talking about either of our pasts. I get the hang of turning the car on pretty quickly, enough that Mavis thinks I can drive around the parking lot to get a feel for the gas.

"And please god, remember that the brake is the left pedal and not the right one," she says. "I know the car is old, but I'd really rather not explain to my parents that it's been crashed into the side of the school."

"Noted," I say, and very hesitantly put my foot on the gas. The car crawls along.

"You can go a little faster than that, Sid," Mavis says, and I slowly accelerate until I'm comfortable, doing circles just around the parking lot. I finally put the car in park and laugh, exhilarated.

"I'm driving!" I say, and impulsively reach over and hug Mavis, as much as I can while we're still both seated. "Thank you."

"Don't thank me too much. You're not allowed on the road yet," Mavis says, but she laughs. I pull back from her and for a split second I see her gaze flit down to my mouth before she looks back up.

"I should . . . I should let you drive home then," I say. "It's getting late."

"Yeah," she says. "If you ever want to do this again, let me know. No one really cares if I borrow the car." She smiles sadly, and on impulse, I reach out and squeeze her hand.

On the drive home, though, that same regret I saw in her face surfaces in my gut. This is something I was supposed to learn with Dad, or Mom if she'd stayed. Not a girl from my class whose parents don't care about her.

If we had to both be fucked over by the universe, though, I'm glad at least we're together.

Dawn Schaefer: February 28, 2008

I FEEL like I know more about Dawn Schaefer than I do any of Dad's other victims. I know she was the lead in the musical and sang alto in the school choir, that she was a better student than I'll ever be and that her birthday was only a week after mine. That the day before she died she found out she'd gotten accepted to the musical theatre program at the University of Michigan.

Of all the girls my father killed, she's the ghost who's visited me the least. I wonder if it's because my father took so much from her.

Or maybe she just has nothing to say to me.

She was never a girl who made good choices. She always wanted to be, sure, and everyone thought she was. Did. Captain of the cheer squad, lead in the school musical. A bright, shining girl with potential.

A boy like Johnny Pritchard is *not* a good choice. Not for

a girl with potential. Her mother hates him, thinks the whole family is trash. Her brother hates him, too, and she's seen the scowl on Jeremy's face any time Johnny is brought up.

It's not her fault Johnny's father, Frank, owns the gas station. Not her fault Johnny works there on weekends and at the Piggly Wiggly on weeknights to save up so he can get out of this shit town. She thinks it means he's hardworking, dedicated, focused. Her mother thinks it means he's a deadbeat who can't get a better job.

He's supposed to pick her up after rehearsal today. Well, technically Jeremy is supposed to pick her up, but she doubts he will. He hates the school musical. She thinks it's just because his ex, Chrissy Swift, is playing the Wicked Witch.

But she knows that on opening night he'll be there right in the front row, along with the rest of her family.

No, her real plan is to go out to Cardinal Lake with Johnny and spend a few hours with him in the back of his truck. If Jeremy does show up and gets pissed, she'll make up an excuse about a late rehearsal, or about staying to help one of the girls run lines.

No one would ever think perfect Dawn Schaefer would lie about *anything*. Even if Jeremy does sometimes suspect.

She waves goodbye to her friends after rehearsal, accepts the compliment about her performance from Mrs. Shaw. She doesn't see Johnny's truck, and she sighs, wondering if it's broken down *again*. But she doesn't have a phone she can call him with.

After a few minutes, a car pulls up to where she's standing.

But when the window rolls down, it isn't Johnny. It's a man.

"Wait," she says. "Wait, I know you—"

"I'm friends with the Pritchards," he says. "Johnny's truck broke down and he mentioned he was coming to get you, and since we've met I thought I'd help him out."

Alarm bells are going off in her head. But Johnny's truck *does* break down a lot, and it's not like he'd have any way to tell her if it did.

So she gets in.

She does end up going to Cardinal Lake like she planned, of course.

She just doesn't come back.

Chapter Ten

MAVIS DROPS me off at home, promising to bring my bike back when she picks me up the next morning. I give her a wave, but as she leaves, I'm still thinking about what she said, about her family not seeing her.

On impulse I turn on the computer, search for information—this time not about my dad's victims, or the missing girls from my class, but about Ginny, Mavis's sister.

There are thousands of articles, a subreddit dedicated to just her disappearance, several true-crime podcast episodes. I'm sure Mavis knows about this, but seeing it myself is overwhelming.

I click on image results and am greeted with a smiling photo of a seven-year-old girl who bears an uncanny resemblance to Mavis. They have the same eyes, same smile, same curly hair.

Is this what her parents are reminded of every time they look at her? Is this what Dad's victims' families feel when they look at their remaining children? This loss? They're stuck, unable to move on from what's happened to their daughters.

Can I blame them, though?

I search for the names of Dad's victims again, trying to find any information about them that isn't connected to their deaths. Melissa Wagner's sister, Cassie, blogged for a while about her experience, but the link in the search results is dead, and there's no archive of the pages. I find memorial pages for Alicia Graves and Samantha Markham, maintained by their families. Samantha's hasn't been updated in two years, but Alicia's has a post from just last month.

I wonder if I could contact any of them. If I could talk to them. There's no contact form on Samantha's page. Alicia's has an email, but it's a university email address, and whoever runs it has definitely graduated by now.

Maybe I could ask Sally Louise for their contact info so I could reach out. She could get it from her dad's files, I'm sure.

"What would that solve?" Savannah asks. She's sitting on the edge of my bed now. June isn't with her. "Would it just make you feel better?"

I don't answer her, though I know she's right. But I just want to talk. To say I'm sorry, because my dad never will.

If the whole town is going to see me as him, anyway, shouldn't something good come out of that?

God, I'm so scared I'm like him.

I'm so scared I'm like him, and I can't talk to the one person who could tell me I'm not. I can't bring it up to her, not after what she told me, not after what happened to her sister.

I have to get through this alone.

True to her word, Mavis presents me with a fixed bike the next morning when she picks me up, even though she still insists on driving us to school. Lilah still hasn't been found. Rumors aren't flying around like they did for Savannah, the gravity of the situation setting in too much. Lilah is most likely dead, but if we say that out loud it'll feel like we just made it happen. Savannah's funeral is in a few days, but it's private. None of us will go, except maybe Craig.

I find Sally after school. She's at her car, keys in hand, when I come up to her.

"Hey," I say. "Are you still on to drive me this weekend?"

"Of course," she says, and turns. "What else do you want?"

"I'm not—"

"Sid, we haven't spoken in years. I know you don't just want to talk," she says.

"Whose fault is that?" I ask, and she sighs. For a moment I think she's not going to answer me.

"My dad's, probably," she says. "Hard to be friends with the person whose dad arrested yours, huh?"

"A judge officially ruled *my* dad is the one at fault here, actually," I say. It's gallows humor, but she cracks a smile at it. "Speaking of . . . Dad's victims' families. The Wagners and Schaefers and Markhams and . . . and the others. Would your dad know where they live?"

Sally's eyes immediately narrow. "Why?"

"I—I want to talk to them. Reach out, ask if—"

"You're the last person those people would ever want to talk to," Sally Louise says. "Sid. You have to know that."

"I know," I say, my face burning. "I just thought . . ."

She shakes her head. "I'm helping you with a lot, Sid, but I'm not going to help you with that. They deserve to move on."

I don't know what to say to that, so I just stand there until Sally gets in her car and drives off.

I have to do something. This is my fault. All of it. I have to do something to atone, and I'm stuck on next steps until I talk to Dad tomorrow. But reaching out is something I can do now, isn't it?

I pull my phone out of my pocket and on impulse open the podcasts app, look at *Dawn of Justice*, at the three episodes listed there. In the show notes for each there's an email for the podcast—I guess so people can reach out with more information, or stories about Dawn.

I tap the link for the email and begin to type.

Dear Jeremy,

I hope this gets to you, or maybe it won't, maybe someone else runs this now. My name is

I stop. What name do I put? Mine? My dad's? There's a

chance as soon as he sees my last name he won't read the rest of the message, anyway.

My name is Sid Atkinson. Dennis Crane is my father.

I wanted to say I'm sorry. I know it probably doesn't mean much. I know it won't bring your sister back. But I'm sorry all the same. Dawn sounds like she was a wonderful—

I stop. That sounds hollow.

I didn't know Dawn. All I know is what I heard on your podcast. It sounds like she was a wonderful sister. And I'm sorry. I'm sorry my dad killed her. I'm sorry he won't ever say that to you, so I will. I know it doesn't change anything. If you ever finish the podcast, even if it's just more about Dawn's life, I'd listen.

How do I end this? What else am I supposed to say except that I'm sorry? That doesn't even begin to cover it. I can't say this shouldn't have happened, because of course it shouldn't have.

Dawn should still be here.

—Sid Atkinson

Before I can stop myself, I hit send. It's only once I do that the regret floods in. Maybe Sally was right, maybe I was only doing this for myself. Maybe I'll get lucky and the email won't be valid anymore.

I don't dare to think about any sort of best-case scenario—that Jeremy sees it and forgives me, forgives my dad. I know that won't happen.

I don't think I forgive my dad, either. And I don't think I ever will.

Maybe that'll be enough, to live with that. But I don't know.

Chapter Eleven

GRAM POKES her head in my room Friday night. For a second I think she's going to tell me to go get pork rinds, but she just stands there in the doorway, her arms folded, until I finally look up from my homework at her.

"Gram?"

"You ready for tomorrow?" she asks. I swallow. I hadn't wanted to tell her that I was going to visit Dad, but she needed to know. It didn't feel right to keep it from her, even if all she did when I told her was sigh.

"Yup."

"Got your clothes ready?"

I make a face, but I nod. I've got an old pair of jeans and a blouse that's more feminine than anything I currently wear. When I was younger and Gram would take me, she'd make me wear a dress, which I hated but understood why she insisted on, especially with my shaved hair.

"Who's taking you?"

"Sally Louise."

"The sheriff's daughter?" Her eyebrows shoot up. "Didn't realize y'all had gotten so close again."

"Yeah, well," I say. I turn back to my homework—which I'm actually doing this time—and think that's going to be the end of it when there's a weight on the end of my bed. I startle, worried that it's June, but it's not. It's just Gram.

"Sid," she says. "What're you hoping to get out of this visit?"

My mouth goes dry. I've been careful not to let her catch on to the fact I'm trying to figure out what's happening now so I can stop it. I know what she'd say—that it's not my responsibility, that I need to keep myself safe.

But it is. She's the one person who might understand that and I can't tell her.

"I . . . I want to talk to him in person."

"About what?"

"About why he did it," I say. I can't meet her eyes. She sighs, and her hand finds mine. Her skin is cold, the rings she always wears heavy.

"Sid," she says. "Don't try to figure him out. It ain't gonna help anything. It's not gonna make you suddenly understand him, or him you." She squeezes my hand. "I don't want you to spend your life waiting for your daddy to love you. He's not capable. Your mother figured that out right away and left. I spent eighteen years raising that boy only to look in his eyes one day and know he wasn't capable of feeling love. I thought he was, when he had you. I thought he might be. But he isn't. And it breaks my heart to say that to you."

I sit there, stunned. It's more than she's said about Dad in years. Ever.

"I know," I say, and my voice is tight. "That's not . . . I know, Gram," I say, and on impulse I throw my arms around her, bury my face in her neck.

"Thank you," I whisper, and I don't know quite what I'm thanking her for—for raising me? For trying the best she could?

I wonder if I'm a second chance for her, but I don't dare ask her that.

I pull back. I can't read her expression, and I worry that she's going to tell me not to go, and that this time I'm actually going to listen to her.

But she doesn't. She just says, "You call me tomorrow if you need anything," and I nod.

"You'd drive on the highway?"

"I ain't gonna take you, if that's what you're thinking," she says. "But if you needed me I'd be there." I can tell she's serious. "Get some sleep, all right?"

"All right," I say, and she leaves. I'm about to cut the lights off, when my phone rings. I glance down at the screen, and my heart begins to pound faster. It's Sally Louise.

"Hello?" I ask as I pick it up. There's nothing for a few beats except for her ragged breathing in my ear. For a second I worry it's not her, it's someone else and she's been taken, but then her voice breaks and it is her.

"Sid," she says, and she's fully crying now, "they found Lilah."

"Oh my god," I say. "Where?" Though in my gut I already know.

"Cardinal Lake," she says.

"Is she—"

"She's dead, Sid," Sally says, and then she starts sobbing so loud I have to hold the phone away from my ear.

"Oh god, Sally, I'm so sorry—"

She sniffs, and I give her a minute, my head reeling. *Lilah is dead. Lilah Crenshaw.*

"Sally, I'm so sorry," I say again, even though it feels inadequate, because what am I supposed to say? Lilah Crenshaw is dead and I didn't even *like* her but she's dead—

She's dead because of me. Someone is copying my dad, and Lilah Crenshaw is dead because of me.

"I can't—I can't help you," she says, and it takes me a minute to remember who's speaking, that it's Sally. "Tomorrow. I can't drive you to the prison, my dad doesn't want me going anywhere." The implication is clear enough: *My dad doesn't want me going anywhere* with you.

"I get it," I say. "I understand. And I—god, Sally, I really am so fucking sorry."

"I know, Sid," she says. "I know you are. Look, I—I have to go, okay? Dad wants me to be there with Lilah's family, and I . . ." She sniffs. "I just have to go."

"Okay," I say, and she hangs up, and I stare at the phone for a long minute before realizing she has.

Lilah is dead. And now I have to talk to my father, now more than ever, because he'll be able to tell me what happens next. Someone's already targeting me, and as the thought crosses my mind, the pain in my ribs twinges. He'll be able to tell me what to do so I can stop this from happening.

There's only one other person I can ask to take me.

I find Mavis in my contacts and pull up her number, calling before I can give myself time to second-guess what I'm doing.

"Sid?"

"Hi," I say, realizing only too late that it's the first time I've ever actually called this girl. "Um. Hi. Mavis?"

"Yeah," she says. "Yeah. It's Mavis. What's up?"

I picture her in her room, lying on her bed, art supplies scattered around her. She said her topic was grief, and for the first time I wonder if it's about her sister. "I . . . I'm so sorry to ask this, but I need a favor."

"You need all of my notes for *Jane Eyre*."

"It's not that," I say. "I need you to drive me somewhere tomorrow."

"Where?"

"Central Prison."

Silence.

"I . . . I need to visit my dad," I say. "I mean. I have an appointment to visit my dad. Gram can't drive me. She won't go on the highway, and my other ride . . . fell through." I don't tell her about Lilah. It's not my news to tell. "I wouldn't ask if I had anyone else," I say. "I'm sorry."

She's quiet for a long moment.

"I'll do it," she says. "But I'm not going in with you."

"I know. I don't want you to. I just—I just need you to drive me. You can drop me off at the entrance and I'll . . . I'll call you when I'm done. It won't be more than an hour, and we can come straight back after."

I shouldn't be asking her this. Not after what happened to her sister.

"Okay," she says. "I'll see you tomorrow."

"Yeah. See you," I say, and hang up before I can convince myself of how awful an idea this really is.

I'm nervous the next morning, changing in and out of the blouse before finally accepting that I have to wear it and pulling it back on. I get Gram to help me take a fresh pair of clippers to my hair before I take a shower, because if I'm going to do this, I'm going to at least try to feel like myself.

I don't think about my dad while Gram cuts my hair. Try not to think about June, or Savannah, or Lilah. At least she hasn't shown up as a ghost yet. I don't think I could take being haunted by her.

Mavis said she'd arrive at noon, and by eleven thirty I'm a nervous wreck, thinking about running to the gas station just so I have some way to burn off all of this nervous energy. But at eleven fifty-five, I hear the sound of tires on gravel, and hurry outside before Gram can call after me to tell me to be safe or something.

"Hey," Mavis says as I get in. Gram waves to us from behind the screen door, and Mavis waves back before turning out of our drive. "You look . . . you look nice."

"Thanks," I mutter. Gram talked me into putting on mascara before I left, and I look at myself in the passenger-side window, frowning. I look like a caricature of a girl, like someone playing dress-up. Thank god I'm at least in pants.

"I mean it," Mavis says. "Do you . . . do you always dress up for this?"

"No," I say. "I . . . it makes it easier. For security. If I look like—if I look like a girl."

"Oh," Mavis says. "Shit. Sorry I asked."

"It's fine," I say. Her phone chirps at her to turn left, and she does, and we speed out of town toward I-40.

Her car is cleaner than the last time I was in it, though there are still a few sketchbooks in the foot. I poke at one of them with the toe of my sneaker, careful not to disturb it, as Mavis turns on the aux system.

We pull up in front of the prison forty minutes later. Mavis drives through the gate, explaining to the guard at the front that I'm here for a visit, and then we're inside. It's the same orange brick it's always been, but that never makes it less intimidating, less terrifying. My father is in here, and men like him, and some men who don't belong in here at all.

Mavis parks the car, kills the engine. "So I'll just . . . I'll just wait for you out here, then?"

"Um . . . you can find a coffee shop if you want. We're close enough to downtown, so there are a lot of good ones."

"Any you recommend?" she asks, and I wince at how *normal* we're trying to make this seem, this girl I might like driving me to see my dad in prison.

"I haven't . . . I've never been to any. So find something for me and tell me about it when you get back," I say, and she looks relieved at this, at being given some task to do that's not waiting around here for me. "It'll probably be an hour, and I'll call you after?"

"Want any coffee or anything?"

"You don't have to—"

"I do," she says, so seriously it makes me want to laugh.

"Surprise me," I say, and she actually smiles as I get out of the car, and for the first time ever visiting my dad, there's this small bubble of hope in my chest, like something today might actually go right.

The walk up to the prison is always my least favorite. The jeans feel restrictive; the blouse is itchy. I hate wearing these clothes. I wish it didn't have to be this way. These visits are humiliating enough. But the stares, the questions, the gender marker on my ID not fully lining up with what they expect me to look like—that would be worse. I'm lucky Gram hates being on airplanes, lucky the last time I flew was when I was still a kid, because airport security would be so much worse now.

The prison looks the same as it always has since I've been visiting Dad. The tall barbed wire, the orange brick that's similar to uniforms. How much time have I spent here? How much time have I spent on the other side of a glass window with a phone pressed to my ear, waiting for some sort of comfort or acknowledgment from my dad that will never come?

I try not to think about Lilah Crenshaw as I walk up to the prison, about her body being found in the lake. About what her last thoughts were, her last moments. We've never liked each other, but that doesn't mean I want her dead. Doesn't mean I want Lilah's family to have to go through that agony.

I hope she's okay. I should call her later tonight, maybe, and see how she is. See if she's holding up.

I tug on my blouse one last time and steel myself. They're going to pat me down. They do every time, and I grit my teeth at the knowledge that it's coming as I walk in the door and greet the guard. He pulls my name from the registry list—my full, legal name—and I pretend I don't hear it even as I hand him my ID that confirms it. I place my phone and wallet in the tray to go through the scanner.

A woman pats me down. She's taller than I am, white no-nonsense face and a hard expression that suggests she's had to do this far too many times and she's not entirely thrilled about it, but what is she going to do?

It's not invasive what she's doing, not really, but it feels like it. Still. It's not half as bad as the way Terry watches me whenever I'm in the gas station.

It's better than what June Hargrove must have felt. Savannah Baunach. Lilah Crenshaw. I try not to think about what they might have felt in their last moments, that wretched intimacy of someone's hands wrapping around their throats.

That has to be how he's killing them. It's what Dad did.

"It hurts," June says. She's perched on the edge of the guard's desk. Her voice is distant, and I stare at her as the female guard pats at my waist. "Being strangled. You don't think it would, but it does."

I don't react. Can't react, and when I finally let myself breathe, when the woman is done with me, June is gone.

I wonder if she'll show up when I'm talking with Dad. If she'll have anything to say. If I were her I'd stay far, far away from this place.

But what would she be afraid of here? She's a ghost.

She isn't real.

Is she?

The guard hands me my laminated pass and I follow her to the main building, clutching my phone and wallet in my hands.

This building looked so big when I was fifteen, the first time I visited. The only time I did with Gram, her hand tight on my shoulder and her lips pressed into a thin line. The visits are always no-contact, and I remember staring at my dad from behind the sheet of plexiglass and not recognizing him.

Gram didn't say a word to him. When they asked if she wanted to speak to him privately without me, she just gave one shake of her head.

He didn't say anything to her, either. What's left to say to each other, when your son kills five girls?

Does she even consider him her son anymore? She and I so rarely talk about him that I've never asked.

I round the corner and there he is. My dad. His hair has thinned significantly since I saw him last, almost two years ago, but when he looks up at me it takes my breath away because it's almost like looking into a mirror. I used to love that, when I was a kid, especially because Mom wasn't around. You could always look at Dad and look at me and tell, instantly, that we were related.

I don't like it now.

It's weird, even now, looking at him, looking into a face that looks like mine. I have Gram's eyes but his mouth, his sharp jawline. The corners of his/my/our mouth constantly pull down. It takes a lot to make either of us smile. We certainly don't during these visits.

Prison has aged my father. It ages most of the men in here, even the ones who, unlike my father, shouldn't be in here to begin with. His hair is completely gray now. When I was a child, it was so brown it was almost black.

Mine is the same color. It would be if I ever gave it a chance to grow.

"Dad," I say. My voice comes out high, and I wince. He doesn't notice, or if he does, he doesn't remark on it.

"Sid," he said. "How's your gram?"

This is not what I expected him to ask. Our visits are never that long, even though they could go for ninety minutes. We usually don't focus on small talk. It's either silence or what his life is like in here. He never asks about mine.

"She's fine," I say.

"She'll be sixty-five this year."

"Not that old."

"No," he says. "Not that old."

He'll be fifty, my dad. In the fall. I'll be eighteen.

"Is she helping look? For the girls?"

The question catches me off guard.

"No," I say. "She—no. She didn't know about the search party for June and with Savannah, she didn't . . . there was a search party but she wasn't part of it." Their names stick in my mouth.

Does he see them, too?

Do they haunt him, too?

I don't think they do. He would have to feel remorse. Something for a haunting to work. That's why they follow me instead.

"Why are—why is this happening again? Why now?" I blurt.

"I don't know that, Sidney," he says, and I bristle at the name because he knows, he *knows* it's Sid now.

"You have to know," I say. "It's because of you. Someone is copying *you*. They're trying to—to send a message or something."

"You think it's me that message is for?" he asks. For the first time, real worry crosses his face. I don't know why he's worried, what he's afraid of, but it just makes me angrier.

"Who else would it be?" I ask. I'm feeling mean. "No one else in our town murdered five girls."

"Why would it be for me, Sid?" he asks. "I'm not even there to see it."

"No, but—"

But I am.

"It's for me," I say. "Isn't it? That's what you're worried about—that the message is for me."

"I'm not worried the *message* is for you, Sid," he says. "I'm worried it *is* you. Girls go missing and someone's copying me? Who do you think the last one they kill is going to be?"

It's the same thing Savannah Baunach said. But it scares me more coming from him. Savannah could be my own paranoia, even though I'm seriously beginning to doubt that. Coming from Dad, though . . .

I flinch. "I'm not a girl." It's the only thing I can hang on to right now. I came here to talk to him about the possibility of me being the last victim, but now that he's confirmed it, now that I have to stare that possibility in the face, I can't bring myself to ask him how I protect myself. It's too close to home.

"I know," he says. "Look. I don't want you mixed up in this."

"You can't tell me someone's probably targeting me and then tell me not to get mixed up in it," I say, and this time I do let my anger take over. "And I wouldn't be *mixed up in this* if it wasn't for you."

I stare at him.

"If I'm next—"

"You won't be next," he says, and the certainty in his voice infuriates and terrifies me.

"How do you know that?"

"Because that wouldn't send a message," he says. "You'll be last."

The cold, matter-of-fact way he says it cuts me to the bone. I can't breathe. For a second I think it's one of the girls, June or Savannah or Lauren, wrapping her hands around my throat, but no. They wouldn't come in here. They wouldn't be so close to him.

"What do I do to stop it?" I ask, though I already know the answer. Find out who's killing the girls. Stop him.

"You can't, Sid."

"So I'm just going to die?"

"No," he says. "You leave it to Grant Kepler to figure out, and you hope he arrests the right guy before he gets to you. Or you convince Marybeth to leave town, and another girl dies instead of you. But I'm telling you to stay out of it."

"You don't get to tell me what not to *stay out of* anymore," I say. I stand. We still have plenty of time left, but I'm done with this conversation. I'm not going to get anything useful out of him.

I'm almost about to set the phone down when a thought strikes me, and even though I don't want to know the answer, I have to ask. I have to know.

"Would it work?" I ask, and he looks at me, the barrier of glass separating us. "If this is someone's idea of revenge, if I'm the last one—would it even make a difference to you?"

He doesn't answer, and that is answer enough.

Samantha Markham: March 4, 2008

DAD'S LAST victim was a girl named Samantha Markham whose younger brother was a grade ahead of me. His family moved the summer after she died, and I never saw them again.

Samantha was found a week after she disappeared. Dad got careless with her, I think; reports said she was only unconscious when she hit the water, not dead like the other girls.

I wonder if her brother thinks about that—this chance that she could have survived, that if my father had not weighted her body down she could have tried to swim back to the surface.

I wonder if it haunts him like his sister haunts me.

A girl goes for a run. Normally she wouldn't, not when the sun is setting, but she had play rehearsal and then homework and now's the only time she can, if she wants to stay in shape for track. Coach has said he's already had recruiters calling about her. The thought makes her beam with pride, but what's better is it'll get her a scholarship, get her out of here.

But not if she lets her form slip, not if she lets any of the girls on the team become faster than her. She's not captain, but maybe next year she will be.

One year left. That's what she keeps telling herself—that she only has one year left before she's out of this school, this town, off to somewhere bigger.

When she leaves, she won't tell anyone she's from Cardinal Creek, North Carolina. She won't be the one from "that town of murdered girls." It's bad enough when she sees a friend now from another high school; all they can talk about—all anyone wants to ask her about—is how it feels, to have four girls from your school murdered.

Fucking scary, she says. But they just nod like they get it, and she wants to scream at them that they don't, but that wouldn't be the polite thing to do.

She thinks about them every day. Dawn and Alicia and Melissa and Lauren. But Melissa the most, because they were actually friends, their siblings almost the same age.

This is going to fuck up her brother for life, she knows. He keeps staring at her like he can't believe she's real, like any minute he thinks Samantha is going to disappear, too, like the rest of the girls. No matter how much Sam reassures him that she's not going anywhere.

This is why she runs. Mostly to get out of her own head, because if she's thinking about the forest under her sneakers she's not thinking about the girls from her town, missing, mourned, betrayed.

Her dad didn't want her to go on this run. Almost forbade her from doing it. She could tell he wanted to. But he didn't. She's heard the warnings from him, can't stop hearing the warnings from him, from everyone, but she also knows that Melissa, Dawn, Lauren, Alicia—they'd want her to keep living her life. They'd want her to get that scholarship and get the fuck out of this town. Because now they're stuck here forever.

She doesn't tell anyone this, of course. Knows it would make her look selfish. It probably is selfish.

She picks up her pace and nears the lake, skids to a halt as she nearly collides with a man coming out of the woods.

"Jesus," she says, and he looks at her.

"What're you doing out here?" he asks.

She should keep running. She starts to keep running—she can outrun him, she knows she can—because something definitely feels wrong here.

But he's faster than she is. Surprisingly fast. He has his arm around her neck before she can even think, and all the while he's whispering in her ear, "I'm sorry, I'm sorry, I didn't want to do this."

She is the final girl to be murdered by Dennis Crane.

She is the final body to be pulled out of Cardinal Lake until June Hargrove in 2018.

Chapter Twelve

I TAKE several minutes in the women's bathroom at the prison to calm down before I head out to the car. No one even looks at me as I collect my stuff and leave. I'm sure they're used to this. I'm sure they see kids like me every day.

Then again, maybe they don't. Some of these men are in prison for things far worse than what my father did. I bet their kids don't even visit.

Sometimes I think I should stop. Cut off all contact, tell Gram I just don't want to anymore. I'm sure she'd understand. I'm sure everyone would understand.

But he's my *dad*. And I know some people say that shouldn't matter, but he raised me for the first thirteen years of my life. All of my childhood memories are with him. Shouldn't that mean something?

I spot Mavis's car from across the parking lot and head toward it, smiling as she waves me down. As soon as I open the door I smell something that smells an awful lot like hot chocolate.

"It's sipping chocolate. There's a cute little chocolate factory near the train station," she says. "I thought you might like it."

I take a sip and make a face, which she laughs at. It's rich, like drinking a straight melted bar of chocolate.

"It's good," I say, and she laughs again, and that sound, after the time I just spent in the prison, does something to me.

"Take it slow," she says. "It's, like, way sweeter than I'm used to. Didn't think you'd even have a place that sells this here."

"Raleigh's not as backwoods as Cardinal Creek," I say. "Pretty sure half the people who live here ain't even from North Carolina."

"It's cute when you say *ain't*," she says, and starts the car. "So how . . . how did it go?"

For a moment I'm too busy short-circuiting at the fact she said something I do is cute to register the question.

"It was . . . fine," I say. She looks like she doesn't want to hear more, though, and I'm not sure if I want to tell her.

"Did you get anything helpful?"

I swallow. I can't tell her I didn't, that the only thing I got from him was the confirmation that I'm going to be the last one killed.

"Not really," I say. I take another sip of my chocolate. It's not as rich this time; I can taste the bitter notes in it, too. "Actually can we just . . . can we just go somewhere else? Please? I don't really want to go home just yet."

There's a hand on the back of my neck and for a second I think it's Mavis, but it's far too cold.

"You don't get to be distracted, Sidney," June whispers in my ear. "You have a responsibility—"

I don't want it, I think suddenly, vehemently. No matter how much I just told Dad he doesn't tell me what to get mixed up in anymore. Why *should* finding the missing girls be my responsibility? Why isn't the sheriff doing anything? Why isn't anyone else *doing* anything?

"Sure," Mavis says, cutting through my thoughts, June's voice. "Where do you want to go?"

She pulls out of the parking lot and I think.

"The movies," I say. I don't know what caused me to say it. I haven't been to the movies since I was a kid, but suddenly I'm desperate to go sit in a darkened theater for a few hours and only focus on the drama on-screen in front of me, not on the fact that three girls have been murdered and I don't know who the next one will be.

"Okay," Mavis says, and quickly searches for movie theaters in the maps app on her phone. "There's one a few miles from here. That work?"

"Yeah," I say. "That works." She smiles at me and starts down the road, and I take another sip of chocolate and look out the window.

All I can taste now is the bitterness.

◆ ◆ ◆

The movie theater is almost empty by the time we pull up, even though it's a Saturday afternoon. But it's too late for the matinee and not late enough for anyone trying to catch an evening show. We see an ad for a special showing of some old movie from the fifties called *The Blob*, which Mavis insists on. I go along with her. The time is right, and it's better than our other options, which are a romance and an action movie about a woman searching for her missing daughter that hits just a little too close to home right now.

I balk, though, when we go up to the counter to buy tickets. Shit. Movies have gotten far more expensive than they were when I was a kid.

"Sid," Mavis says, when she notices I'm stalling, "let me get it."

"I—"

"My treat," she insists, and I stuff down all of my thoughts about how she shouldn't and how it's unfair because she's paid for me before, and she drove me all the way out here—

"Go call your gram so she doesn't worry," Mavis says, noticing the expression on my face, and I can't tell if it's because she actually thinks that's a good idea or if she knows I'll start protesting about the tickets if I stand near her too long.

"Fine," I say, and head to a quiet corner of the lobby. Gram picks up immediately.

"Yello?"

"Hey," I say. "Um. I'm at the movies. With my friend. We'll

be home later. I didn't want you to worry."

There's a long silence on the other end of the line before Gram says, "Have fun," in this tone of voice that sounds like she knows about my crush. I groan. "Bring back some popcorn if y'all don't eat it all."

"Yes, ma'am," I say, and hang up. Popcorn. Shit. I forgot that would cost money, too.

But by the time I find Mavis, she's already standing at the counter, holding a bucket of popcorn and a soda the size of a small child.

"Didn't know what you'd want, but everyone likes popcorn, right?" she asks. "And I got us a Coke we could split." It's only then I notice the two straws sticking out of the Coke.

"Sure," I say, and she grins, and I follow her into the theater.

It's freezing cold in the theater. We're the only people besides this couple who look like they're both about Gram's age. With a start I realize it's two butch women, both with tan white skin and almost identical short salt-and-pepper hair. Some sort of recognition bubbles up in me, these women who look somewhat like me when I *never* see anyone who looks like me where I live.

And then the movie starts and Mavis and I are immediately giggling, because it's supposed to be this terrifying horror film but the theme song for the movie sounds almost cheerful, straight out of the 1950s.

Beware of the blob, it creeps, and leaps, and glides, and slides across the floor. . . .

"Shh," Mavis shushes me once the song repeats and I start humming along to the chorus. I laugh, and she takes the opportunity to put a piece of popcorn in my mouth before turning back to the screen.

God, I can't believe we're doing this. That I get this. That I even deserve something like this, something this good.

"You don't."

It's June. I try to ignore her, try to focus on what's happening in front of me on the screen, where two teenagers—or are they thirty, it's really hard to tell—are trying to convince the town doctor to help the old man they've found whose hand is now covered in a strange goo.

All through the movie I keep sneaking glances at Mavis. Two rows up, one of the women leans her head on the other's shoulder, and I wish I was her, I wish I could be her. It doesn't matter that she has problems just like I do, that I don't know who she is. She is not me, and for the moment that's enough.

But Mavis is here next to me, and maybe that could be enough, too. She laughs at a scene in the movie, some joke I've totally missed, and then catches me looking at her. Without a word she reaches over and takes my hand, giving it a squeeze.

I try to get lost in the movie, in the feeling of this girl's hand in mine. She laughs again, and it's a sound I wish I could keep but one I know I don't deserve.

Something else takes my other hand. Something wet. Something rotting. I glance to my right, and there is June. When she smiles, half her teeth are missing.

"Bathroom," I mumble to Mavis, and stand up so suddenly I almost knock over the bucket of popcorn. I run out into the lobby, choosing the women's' restroom before I have time to think it over, gripping the edges of the sink.

"What's the matter, Sid?" June asks. She cocks her head, laughs. "I thought you wanted someone to hold your hand."

"You're not real," I say. "If you were real you'd just tell me who killed you, and I could be done with this."

"But you haven't earned it yet," she says. She leans over me so her rotting breath is tickling my ear and runs a finger down the glass of the mirror. It leaves a mark.

"I'm real," she whispers, "and you'd better find out who killed me, or I'm never going to leave you alone. Ever." She smiles and in an instant she's gone, leaving nothing but a streak down the mirror.

I wish my dad's victims would show up. It's a terrible thought, but as I'm standing there gripping the sink in the bathroom of the movie theater, all I can wish is that they would show up and tell me how long I need to atone for him for, because I'm worried it's going to be the rest of my life.

◆ ◆ ◆

"That was fun," Mavis says as we exit the theater. It's dark already, and a biting February chill has settled in the air. I wish I'd thought to bring a jacket, but then again, I didn't think I'd be out this long after speaking with Dad.

"It was weird," I say. "I don't know if I'd call it fun."

She starts humming the theme song as we walk to the car. "No, but I think torturing you with this song is going to be fun."

"You're the worst," I say, but I'm laughing as we get into the car.

"Maybe I am," she says. She opens her maps app again and pulls out of the parking lot. "But you had fun, yeah?"

"Yeah," I say. "Yeah, I had fun."

We get to my house forty minutes later. Any embarrassment I felt this morning at Mavis pulling up and seeing where I live has evaporated. She's already driven me to prison. Our trailer is nothing.

Neither of us said anything when we passed the billboard with Lilah's face on it. We pretended not to notice.

"Hey, Sid?" Mavis says, just as I'm about to get out of the car.

"Hmm?"

"I had—I had a good time. With you. Even . . . well, even with everything else happening," she says. Her gaze flicks down to my lips, then back up. "Um, can I . . . can I kiss you?"

"Yes," I say, and for a second I don't think she hears me but she must have because she's leaning toward me, and then her lips brush my own and it's soft and sweet and leaves me aching. When I pull back, she's smiling.

"That was okay?" she asks.

"Better than okay," I say, and she laughs. I want to keep that sound inside my bones forever, even if it feels like it's not allowed right now.

"I'll see you Monday," she says.

"Monday," I echo, and wave to her again as I get out of the car.

I can't stop smiling as I head inside. Even Gram notices.

"How was your movie?" she asks, that sly smile on her face. "What'd y'all go see?"

"*The Blob*," I say, and she laughs.

She doesn't ask about my visit, and normally I'd press her to, but I'm so caught up in kissing Mavis, in this feeling of something finally going right for once.

"You and that girl have a good time?"

"Yeah, Gram," I say. "We had a good time."

Chapter Thirteen

ON MONDAY, Mavis persuades me to try to eat in the lunchroom with her, if only because it's so cold outside. I'm not sure I'm ready to brave eating together in the lunchroom, all the stares, especially since I don't even know what we *are*. She met me in the parking lot this morning so we could walk in together, and my face was hot the entire time. The news vans haven't come back; briefly I wonder if Principal Johnston finally banned them from campus.

Sure enough, the second I step inside I feel overwhelmed. I'm about to back out, tell Mavis I'll just eat outside in the freezing cold, or maybe we can even eat in her car, when I spot Sally Louise. She's sitting alone at a table in the back, looking small, and I realize it's because Lilah's not with her, because Lilah was always the loud one, the one who drew people to her, and without her, Sally Louise is just lost. People may like Sally Louise, but no one wants to be close friends with a girl whose dad is the sheriff. They're too afraid she might run off and report them.

No one wants to be friends with someone whose dad is a killer, either.

"I'll be right back," I tell Mavis, and walk up to Sally's table. I can feel everyone's eyes on me as I do so, which just reaffirms my decision to eat outside.

"Sally?"

She looks up. She looks even worse than last week, like she hasn't slept at all. She probably hasn't.

"Can I sit down?" I ask her, and she just shrugs. I take a seat across from her. She doesn't react, just goes on picking at her lunch.

"Are you okay?" I ask.

She scoffs. "Do I look okay?"

"No," I say. "You look like shit."

She laughs, loud enough people turn to look at us. "You're the only person who'll say that, so thanks, Sid," she says. "Well. You and Lilah would have, if she was—"

"I know," I say. "Look, I . . . I wanted to say I'm sorry. For getting you involved. For Lilah getting killed."

"That's not your fault," Sally Louise says immediately, and this time her eyes do meet mine. "You know that, right? Lilah got killed because of some sick fuck, not because of you."

"Sally . . ."

"It's true," she says. She straightens up. "And I would've

gotten involved either way, so—so you can take your apology back for that, too. This isn't going to deter me, Sid. He needs to pay." She sets her jaw, and she looks exactly like her dad in that moment.

"I know," I say. "I know he does. I'll make sure of it."

"I believe you," she says. She sighs, and I think that's the end of it and start to get up, but she stops me.

"Sid," she says. "I don't need your apologies, but I think you should go to the funeral. You owe it to Lilah."

"I don't think anyone wants me there," I say, thinking of Mrs. Crenshaw that day in the hallway.

"It's not about them. It's about what Lilah would have wanted."

"You think Lilah would have wanted me there?" It's my turn to scoff. "She didn't even like me."

"I think deep down she might have."

"Deep down doesn't matter when that's not what she showed me," I say, and Sally shrugs again.

"You owe her," she repeats, and I know she's right. It's my fault Lilah Crenshaw is dead, even if Sally Louise doesn't see it that way. It's my father's fault Sally Louise and I aren't even friends anymore in the first place.

"I'll go," I say. "It's tomorrow, right?"

"Yeah," she says. "In the evening. Her voice breaks on the last word, and I push back from the table, leaving Sally alone with her grief, no ghost even to reassure her.

◆ ◆ ◆

Mavis is still standing at the entrance to the lunchroom, leaning on the wall and munching on an apple.

"Sorry," I say. "That took longer than I thought."

"What were you talking about?"

"We were just talking about Lilah's funeral," I say. No sense in telling her I was apologizing for Lilah's death. She doesn't want to be involved, and I don't want to bring it up to her, knowing what she's been through.

"Are you going to go?"

"I am," I say. "It's tomorrow. You're welcome to come. You did know her."

Mavis shakes her head quickly. "No. I don't want to. I'm surprised you're . . ." She bites her lip, trails off.

"We don't have to talk about it," I say. "In fact, I'd rather not. I'd rather go eat in your car and talk about driving." I give her a quick smile, hope it's reassuring. I can't tell if it is or not.

"All right," she says. I fall into step beside her as we walk to her car. "Explain to me how you start a car."

I roll my eyes, but I do, even sitting in the driver's seat once we reach her car. The rest of the time we spend eating is comfortable enough, though I can't shake the feeling every time I look in the rearview mirror that Lilah's going to be waiting for me.

"Want to meet up after the funeral?" I ask. "Diner's open for dinner, and I've got cash. Let me treat you for once."

"Like a date?" Mavis asks, and my face heats up.

"Yeah," I say. "Like a date. We can even . . . we can make plans for Valentine's, if you want to."

"Sounds good," Mavis says. "Just text me when the funeral's over and I'll meet you there."

The bell rings, and she kisses me on the cheek when we get out of the car.

For once, I don't care if anyone's looking at me.

Lilah's funeral is packed. I can't tell if there's more people here than there were for June, since then I could only judge by the number of cars in the parking lot. The Baptist church has been getting a lot of traffic recently because of the girls, even with Savannah's funeral being private. The funeral parlor must be doing well.

It's a sick thought, but I can't stop myself from thinking it.

I slip in the back just before the service starts. Maybe I'll get lucky; maybe no one will recognize me.

But as soon as I think that, I spot Sally Louise, walking in with her parents. She glances at me and smiles, but it looks pasted on. At least she knows I'm here, though. At least I showed up.

I zone out as the funeral itself begins. In front of me are two guys, their heads bent together, and I realize with a start that I know them. Terry and Johnny.

Who invited them?

But it's a public affair, so most likely they're here just to gloat, to gawk. It's not like they knew Lilah. Or Savannah. Or June.

Why are they here?

Now would be a great time for June to show up, or Savannah, or Lilah, someone who can fucking solve this for me and tell me if I need to worry about the two guys who are sitting in the row in front of me or if I'm really just being paranoid.

I stare at them through the entire service, wondering if I've had it all wrong and the killer isn't some mysterious person I need to find but someone I know, someone right in front of me. They're about as outcast as I am and maybe I shouldn't blame them, but if they killed her—

But they're quiet during the funeral. I can't see their faces, Johnny or Terry, but there's no whispering, no laughter, nothing that would make me think something's up.

I still want to know why they're here.

I text Mavis as soon as the funeral ends, telling her I'll be at the diner in a minute. And then I put my phone on vibrate and try, as inconspicuously as possible, to follow Terry and Johnny out to the parking lot. It's easy enough; they don't go to the front to try to tell the Crenshaws how sorry they are. We get caught up in the crowd of mourners, but I don't lose sight of them.

They head for a truck parked at the far corner of the lot, and my blood runs cold.

Were they the ones who tried to run me down?

Sheriff Kepler is still inside. I could run in and grab him, but what would I even say? Some guy runs me off the road, doesn't mean he's a killer. I know both brothers and they're assholes and creeps, sure, but killers?

What do I have to go on other than a gut feeling and the fact that a jacket was found near the gas station?

I start to head back inside to tell the sheriff but freeze with my hand on the stair railing. The only evidence I have is the same evidence that Sheriff Kepler already wanted to grill me about. I don't have anything, not really. Not unless I follow them and try to find something.

My phone buzzes insistently in my pocket, and I pull it out. Shit. I'm supposed to be meeting Mavis. I don't have time to follow the Pritchard boys right now.

But surely the QuikMart will be open when I leave. I can always go there then, and try to confront them. Hope that June or Savannah shows up to confirm my suspicions, though I know that's not how it works.

Until then, though, I'll have to be satisfied with the fact that I have a plan.

I hurry over to the diner, that weird sense of déjà vu creeping over me. It's the same place I met Mavis three weeks ago after June's funeral. It doesn't feel like a month ago. It feels like a week. It feels like a lifetime.

It's empty for now—no mourners hanging around. Lilah Crenshaw's parents have money, friends, more so than the Hargroves. Funerals mean casserole dishes around here; they won't have to think about cooking for a week.

Mavis is already inside and sitting down when I enter. Darius is working the counter and waves at me before glancing between Mavis and me and giving me a thumbs-up. I roll my eyes and smile before taking the seat across from Mavis.

"So," I say. "What do you want to eat? My treat."

"You're sure?" she asks. She's changed since school; she's in a soft pink sweater and light blue jeans. I suddenly feel self-conscious about my own hoodie.

"I said it's a date, right?" I ask. "We can . . . we can split a stack of pancakes. They're huge. If you want."

"Pancakes sound great," she says, and I go up and order. When I pull out a few bills to drop in the tip jar, though, Darius shakes his head.

"Please let me at least tip something," I whisper so Mavis doesn't hear.

"It's on the house," he whispers back.

"Gram's not going to like that."

"Marybeth doesn't have to know," he says. I sigh, but put the cash in the tip jar, anyway.

"Don't see how you stay in business," I mutter, and he laughs.

"You can just pay next time you bring your date here," he

says, and I glare at him before he retreats back into the kitchen.

I sit back down, try to smile at Mavis. But my eyes keep darting toward the door, wondering if anyone's going to come in. I tap my fingers on my thigh, trying to see if I can spot the Pritchards' truck from here.

"Are you expecting someone?" Mavis asks. I turn my attention back to her.

"Sorry," I say. "Just . . . just hoping no one from the funeral shows up here."

I can't help but think of last time. Of what Mavis told me, Lilah showing up after I'd left, telling her who I was. From the look on her face, she's thinking about that, too.

"If they do, we'll just leave," Mavis says decisively. "Go back to the pizza place or something." She takes a sip of her water. I do, too, if only to give my hands something to do.

"I've never been on a date," I confess after a minute, once she hasn't said anything. "I don't know what to do."

"I don't either," she says. I take another sip. I don't want to talk about school, or *Jane Eyre*, or anything to do with the girls. But I can't stop myself from looking out the window every few seconds to see if the truck has left yet.

Our food finally comes, saving us from more awkward silence. Darius brings out two large plates, the pancakes in the shapes of hearts. He winks at me when he sets them down.

I'm going to get him for this.

We dig into the pancakes. They're delicious, fluffy and thick, and the syrup tastes real, not fake. I eat a whole quarter of one before Mavis has even finished a few bites.

I'm about to say something about how good they are when movement outside the window catches my eye. The truck, idling slowly down the road. I'm sure it's them.

"Sid."

I look back. Mavis is looking at me like maybe that wasn't the first time she called my name.

"What're you looking at?" she asks. She cranes her neck to see out the window.

"I think that's the truck that ran me off the road," I say. I can't help but say it. She looks back at me.

"Really?"

"I mean, I didn't see the license plate or anything, but they were at the funeral—"

"Is that why you were late?" she asks. "Were you . . . I dunno, investigating the truck or something?"

"I just wanted to see if it was the same one," I say. "And I think it is, but I don't know if that even means anything." I shake my head. "I'm sorry."

"It's okay," she says, and goes back to eating. But now that I've started thinking about the truck, about that day, I can't stop.

And then something catches my eye again, and I turn. I

swear it's her. Lilah. She's staring at me through the window, wearing the same sour expression she always did around me when she was alive.

"Sid," Mavis says, and my attention snaps back to her. "Are you all right?"

I shake my head. "No, I just—I thought I saw Lilah." I turn again, but she's gone.

"Lilah Crenshaw?" Mavis puts her fork down, frowns. "Lilah's dead. You were just at her funeral."

"No, but I . . ." I swallow. "It doesn't matter."

"Sid," Mavis says gently, and she reaches over and squeezes my hand before letting go. "You didn't see Lilah. She's dead. She's not a ghost."

"She is," I insist, before realizing what I've said. "All of them are."

"All of who?"

"The girls," I say, and my voice breaks, because now that I've said it, the words won't stop coming. "All of them. My dad's victims. June. Savannah. I see them. Hear them. And I thought I saw Lilah just now because I haven't—haven't seen her yet but you're right, maybe it wasn't her, but she hasn't showed up yet so I thought if—if I saw her, maybe . . . ," I gasp, and Mavis pushes her water glass toward me.

"You're okay," she says as I take a gulp of it. "Hey. The ghosts aren't real."

"They are," I start to protest, but I stop at the look on her face. I take another drink, a breath, try to calm myself down. Mavis looks uncomfortable.

"When . . . when Ginny went missing, I thought I saw her everywhere," she says softly. "Every day. I thought I heard her voice calling me, or her music turned up when no one was home. But it wasn't her. It wasn't her ghost, or her spirit, or whatever you want to call it. There was nothing there. It was just me, and my guilt."

"That's not—I *feel* them, Mavis. I can smell them rotting. June grabbed my hoodie once and it left a mark," I say. I keep talking, desperate to fill the silence. "I was thinking, what if I . . . what if I reached out to some of them? Their families, I mean."

Mavis's face clouds over. "That's not a good idea, Sid."

"But if it could help . . ."

"Help them, or help you?" she says. "They don't want to hear from you."

It's the same thing Sally Louise said, but somehow it stings more coming from Mavis. I shouldn't have brought it up. I think with guilt about the email I sent Jeremy Schaefer, and wish for a split second that I could unsend it.

Mavis sighs and reaches for my hand again, but this time she hesitates before she takes it, like she doesn't really want to.

"Look," she says. "We . . . we should talk about this later. I think you're more upset about Lilah's death than you realize, and you should let me drive you home."

I deflate. "Okay," I say, and we finish our pancakes quietly and leave. I'm still thinking about the truck, about Lilah, when Mavis drops me off, kissing me on the cheek.

It's only when I'm lying in bed that night, trying to fall asleep, that I realize we didn't even try to plan another date.

Chapter Fourteen

THE NEXT day at lunch, I sit with Sally Louise. Mavis joins us once I wave her down, and Sally only raises an eyebrow.

"Am I your pity project now?" Sally says, but there's only a little malice in it instead of her usual bite. She's still not wearing makeup, but she looks less tired than she has been. She's in a hoodie that could have belonged to me, once.

"No," I say. "Honestly, I just need to study and it's easier to do in here than sitting outside."

"You? Study?" Sally asks incredulously. She turns to Mavis. "Didn't think anyone could get Sid to study."

"I have to," Mavis says, and I blush. "We're partners on *Jane Eyre* together."

"You can join us, if you want," I say. I don't know what makes me say it, maybe the ghost of my nine-year-old self who used to be best friends with Sally. She narrows her eyes like maybe we *are* playing a prank on her, then sighs.

"Fine. But only because if we all fail, we have to repeat this hellish year together and none of us want that," she says. "Though you know, for a second I thought y'all were about to recruit me into your little Mystery Incorporated group."

"I don't know what you're talking about," Mavis says stiffly.

"She's not really involved," I say to Sally Louise. Sally frowns.

"But you're still investigating," she says to me, and it's not a question. "What happened to June and Savannah and Lilah."

Sally Louise has gotten better at hiding her feelings than when we were kids. She doesn't even stumble over Lilah's name.

"Yes," I say. "You could help, if you want—"

"Haven't I helped enough?" she asks, and Mavis looks between us.

"Has she been helping?"

"Some," I say, and Mavis looks surprised by that, but I don't have time to think about that right now. "You said you wanted to find out who did it," I say to Sally. "For Lilah. And you've got access to your dad. To police records and stuff. Maybe whoever's doing it has . . . has some sort of record, or was connected with the murders years ago, or has some connection to the victims now and we could figure out who's going to be next. . . ." I trail off. I don't need to bring up that I know who will be last.

"You want me to steal records from my dad?" This time Sally does sound skeptical. "Don't you think he'd need those? Don't you think he's already spending enough time trying to find these girls? They're trying everything they did last time, Sid, and nothing's coming up."

It took them five years to catch Dad last time, I think. It took them five years to even seriously start looking for the girls, and that was after Sheriff Kepler got the position. He even made it part of his platform, when he ran—that he'd finally find out what had happened.

"Sid, maybe she doesn't want to," Mavis says tentatively. "That's . . . that's asking a lot, don't you think?"

"I . . . you're right. I'm sorry," I say, deflating. Both of them are looking at me now, and I crumple a bit under the scrutiny.

Sally sighs. "Look," she says. "If y'all want to do a little study club at the library tomorrow evening or whatever, I *might* join in that." The bell rings, and she stands. "And I *might* see what files I can bring from the police station without my dad noticing, because he sure as hell isn't going to want me to see *you* again," she says to me. "But only if we actually talk about the damn book we're supposed to be reading—or if either of you need help with calculus." She gives us a smirk, the same one I've seen her give to boys in the hallway to make them go weak at the knees, do whatever she says, and I already know we both will.

Gram is cooking when I get home, and I wonder why. I can smell it immediately, even before I walk in the door—vinegar chicken, her specialty. If she bought a whole chicken, I'm not going to complain. It'll be good to not eat boxed mac and cheese for once.

"Hope you're hungry," she says. "Supper'll be ready in an hour."

"It's four."

"And five is suppertime. I'll be hungry. You can always just pick the skin off later like you do."

"What's the occasion?" I ask. She smiles.

"One of them Pritchard boys from down the road said he was makin' a grocery run and asked if I wanted anything. I promised him I'd fry him up a chicken next week if he'd bring me a whole one tonight."

My mouth goes dry. Pritchard boys.

"Which boy?"

"I cain't keep 'em straight," she says. "The tall one."

"Gram, they're both tall to you. You're under five feet."

"Exactly," she says. "Ain't you got homework to do?"

"Yes, ma'am," I say, and scuttle off to my room. It's hard to concentrate. All I can smell is the chicken, and it reminds me that I barely ate lunch today, since we spent the whole time talking to Sally Louise.

I can't believe she's still helping me. Then again, she knew all the girls who've died, far better than I did. Her dad is the sheriff. Maybe she's got some sense of justice baked into her or something.

Still. I'm not going to complain about her helping. There's something I'm missing, I know it.

Pritchard boys.

But something doesn't feel right about them—if they wanted to fuck with me, they'd do it directly. Or they'd do something to Gram. Does that mean they'd commit murder?

They ran me off the road, though. They could have killed me. I can't ignore that.

"I'm going for a ride," I tell Gram, hurriedly throwing on my hoodie.

"I'll warm up the chicken for you when you get back."

"Thanks, Gram," I say, and then I'm out the door and down the road.

I pedal hard, needing that burning in my legs and in my lungs. I need to feel it. I need to feel something that hurts.

Halfway to the gas station, though, I skid to a stop, right in front of Lilah's billboard, just as common sense cuts in.

What am I doing? What am I going to do when I get there, confront them? Say "How dare you help my gram out and pick up food for her?"?

Say "I think you killed June and Savannah and Lilah. I think you tried to run me over."?

I look up at that damn billboard again. I don't know who keeps changing it out, who has the energy.

Then again. All they need to change is the picture.

See This Girl.

Lilah smiles down at me, like she knows something I don't. The way she always looked at me when she was alive.

I start pedaling again, make it to the gas station in record time. The truck is the only one in the parking lot again, and my anxiety spikes. Cautiously, I walk over to it.

I couldn't see the license plate. It sped off after it clipped me. I don't even know if this is the same truck, for god's sake.

But what if it is?

I'm reaching out for it, not really knowing what I'm doing, when the door to the gas station swings open, and a guy the spitting image of Terry stares at me. He's older, his face somehow even thinner, and I know who it is. Johnny. His older brother.

"What're you doin'?" he asks, heading toward me. I straddle my bike, and he breaks into a run just as I pedal off.

Shit. Shit shit shit.

I don't stop pedaling hard until I reach the billboard again, terrified that at any second I'm going to hear the roar of his truck engine behind me. Any time I hear a car, I swerve off the road. By the time I finally arrive home, my heart is pounding so hard I think it's going to make its way out of my chest.

"Sid?"

Gram looks at me as I come in.

"You all right? You look like you've seen a ghost."

But that's the problem—for once, I haven't. For once, the girls are leaving me alone.

As if they know something's coming.

I bike to the library the next day. Sally wanted us all to meet around 3:30 since her dad's about to put a new curfew into effect—no teenagers allowed out alone at all after six. I got a text from her the night before, just as I was about to fall asleep. I can't believe she actually wants to go through with the study group.

I take the long way to the library, just so I don't go past the gas station again, though by now I'm convinced I've made it all up. All he asked is what I was doing near his truck.

But if I had let him get closer, what then?

Girls live in these what-ifs, I know. I'm enough in the in-between to live in them, too. *What if I had talked back/What if I didn't wear that/What if I was prettier, would he have/What if I had said no/What if what if what if—*

There are no good answers to those *what-ifs*. There never will be.

Mavis is waiting by the circulation desk when I walk inside after chaining my bike up. She smiles when she sees me, and I feel myself blush.

Maybe we can go somewhere after this. If she wants. We still haven't made plans for Valentine's Day.

"Hey," she says.

"Hey yourself."

"Did you do the reading?"

"I actually did," I say, pulling my copy of *Jane Eyre* out of my backpack. Compared to Mavis's copy, it still looks brand-new. Hers is battered and has a ton of sticky tabs sticking out of the pages. "I cannot believe Rochester just hid his wife in an attic."

"You can't?" She raises an eyebrow.

"I can," I say defensively. "But he just . . . it's like he forgets about her."

"Does he?" she counters. "He's brooding about it on, like, every page. It haunts him. That's the point."

"I don't see how Jane can go for that, though," I say. "I mean . . . go for someone who—who keeps something like that from her."

"Don't you?" Mavis asks. I don't answer her. Suddenly I don't think we're talking about *Jane Eyre* anymore.

I take out my phone and look at the time. Three thirty-eight. Mavis glances down at her watch.

"Is Sally Louise usually late to things?"

"Are you kidding?" I ask. "She'd show up at school an hour early if she could." Paranoid thoughts start to worm themselves into my head, but I shove them away. "Do you think . . . ?"

"She's just late," Mavis says, with such certainty that I have to believe her.

Ten more minutes go by. Sally Louise still doesn't show up.

"I'm going to call her," I say, and before Mavis can object, I pack my things and head outside. Sally picks up after the second ring.

"Hello?" She sounds out of breath.

"Hey, it's—it's Sid. We were . . . we thought you were meeting us at the library to study."

"Oh. Shit. Sorry, Sid, I—I totally forgot. Dad wants to go visit his family today. But I'll see you tomorrow."

She hangs up before I can say goodbye, and I'm left staring at the phone in my hand, bewildered.

After a few minutes, Mavis joins me outside.

"What'd Sally say?" she asks.

"She says she forgot. But . . ."

"But," Mavis repeats, and I sigh.

"It's just—it's not like her. She's not forgetful. You don't know her, she's meticulous and plans everything and—" The more I go on, the more the panic rises in my chest. "I think something happened. To her."

"Sid, you just talked to her."

"I know, but—"

"Sid," Mavis says. When I look at her, she looks tired. "I wasn't going to say anything with Sally here, but she isn't, and I think . . . I think you need to stop."

"What are you talking about?"

"The girls, Sid," she says. "You're paranoid. You're obsessed. So much that you said you're *seeing* them. I believe you're haunted, but I don't think it's ghosts, Sid. I think it's guilt."

"Why would it be guilt?"

"You tell me, Sid," she says. "Why would it be? Why do you think it's your job to save these girls?"

"Because my dad—"

"You're *not* your dad, Sid," she says. "Why can't you see that?"

"Because everyone in this damn town thinks I am!" I snap. "Because everywhere I go I'm reminded of him, because no one will let me forget who he is, or what he did. Every single fucking day no one lets me forget it, ever, so I have to find these girls because if I do, then—"

Something in Mavis's face hardens.

"I'm not like him," I say.

"Who are you trying to prove that to? Yourself, or him?" she asks, and it's like a fucking awful punch in the gut. "I don't . . . god. If it were me I would have cut him out a long time ago."

And there it is. The real reason behind this. The reason that's been behind it all along, I think.

"You don't like that I still talk to him," I say. I cannot believe we are having this fight out in front of the library, but there is nowhere else I can think of to do this, and we seem determined or destined to have it here. "That—that he's still in my life."

"Someone murdered my sister, Sid. Of course I don't fucking like it."

"He's my *dad*," I say, and it sounds so weak to my ears even when I say it, because at the end of the day, what does that even mean? To us? He's Gram's son, but she's had no problem cutting him out. Why can't I do the same?

"And she was my sister," Mavis says simply. "I need to go home. I can't . . . I'm sorry. I can't do this."

"What about . . . what about our project?" I ask. I'm grasping at straws, saying it, but it feels like the only thing I can hold on to right now.

"We'll hand it in late," Mavis says, her back already turned to me, already heading to her car. "I'm sure it'll be excused, given everything. I'll see you tomorrow, Sid."

"Mavis . . ."

But she's already shut the door to her car and cranked the engine, and before I can even really fully comprehend it, she's driving off, leaving me and my guilt, not the ghosts, watching her go.

I'm already dreading school, even before I get into homeroom to see Sally's seat still empty—Mavis's, too.

Fine. They're both going to ignore me, then. Fine.

But by second period, Mavis still hasn't shown up. Neither has Sally, and my frantic texts to both of them during the break between classes have gone unanswered.

"They don't want to talk to you," Lilah whispers in my ear

at lunch, where I'm sitting outside again. "Sally never liked you, anyway."

Unlike Savannah, Lilah looks very much the way she did when she was alive. Her head isn't even shaved, and when she catches me looking at it, she laughs.

"Guess this guy thought your dad was too boring to keep copying," she says. "He left me alone."

But how do I know that's right? How do I know what she's saying is real? This Lilah isn't real, she's not, she's just a fucking figment of my imagination, of my guilt made physical, like Mavis said.

"Physical guilt? Oh, that's a new one. Didn't think you were good enough at metaphors to come up with that. I sit next to you in English, you know," she says.

Sit. Sat. I don't comment on the present tense. I can't.

"I wonder," Lilah says, "how long it'll take Sally to start haunting you."

My head snaps up at that. "She . . . I talked to her yesterday. She was fine."

"Mmm. Did she *sound* fine to you, Sid? Did she sound like the girl you've known since you were a child? Because that's what you're always thinking, isn't it? That you know her *so much better* than I do." Her face turns ugly, sneering. "Sally Louise would never be late to something, even something with you. I should know. I'm her best friend."

I can't take this anymore. The paranoia is swirling around

my body, this crushing, aching fear that I can't shake.

I try to call Mavis. The phone rings once, twice, three times. She doesn't pick up, and that anxiety tightens in my chest even further. She could just be ignoring me.

I need, now more than ever, to talk to my father.

I skip the rest of school. My grades are shit enough it doesn't matter now, anyway, not like I ever had plans of leaving this town, of going to California, of doing something with my life.

I call the prison on my cell phone. I have to look up the number and redial it twice because my hands are shaking so much I punch it in wrong the first time.

I get the receptionist and I'm speaking so fast he doesn't understand me. "I need to speak to Dennis Crane. He's an inmate?"

"Inmates can't receive calls. Who is this?"

"It's his—" I swallow. "It's his daughter, please, it's an emergency, I have to talk to him—"

The voice on the other line hesitates.

"Please," I beg. "Please, I have to talk to him. It'll just take a minute—"

"One moment."

The person hangs up and I swear, and when the phone rings again, I nearly drop it. I hurriedly press one to accept the call, the phone held tightly against my ear.

"Dad?"

“Sid,” my dad says, and if he’s surprised, he doesn’t sound like it. “What do you want?”

I take a deep breath, and I ask him what I’ve been afraid to ask before.

“Tell me everything about what you did to the girls.”

Dennis Crane: 2008

HE DOESN'T know when he first gets the idea, this urge to kill the girls. Maybe it's after his wife leaves, or maybe it's always been there, the thought. The rage. White-hot. Even as a kid he had a hard time controlling it. He found out quickly enough it wasn't the kind of thing he could show to anyone. Not his mom, not his sisters. He saw how they shrank back from his own father's rage often enough. And thinking of it as something separate from him made it easier to hide—for a while.

The rage is what caused it. The rage is what made him kill the girls. This separate, insidious thing, flaring up whenever his life was unfair, whenever his wife nagged at him. He thought he'd buried it, but he knows now it was always there, waiting, curled and poised and ready to strike.

It comes in waves. As a kid he'd feel it whenever his sisters excluded him from anything, whenever his mother favored them over him. As a teen, the same, whenever a girl laughed at him, turned him down for a date. It didn't happen often—he didn't ask them out often—but he could feel it all the same.

It went away when he met Julie sophomore year of college. The year he dropped out. When they got married and finally moved in together after she graduated, it came back, because he could feel it surfacing in him with every look she gave him. She thought she was better than him; he could see it in her face.

Then she got pregnant, and for a while, things were all right, even though she had to quit her job and he had to pick up additional shifts at the post office. It's what he's supposed to do, she tells him. Provide. And for the first time he feels superior to her, because he's the one with a job, never mind the fact she's the one with a college degree and he's just a dropout. The superiority wins against the rage, and he's almost able to forget about it for a few years.

Almost.

But Julie has no interest in being a mother once Sidney's old enough to stop being cute, and he feels it coming back then in bits and pieces, particularly when she brings up work, or going back to work, or how much she loathes the idea of being a stay-at-home mother. The rage breaks through any walls he's built up, and it becomes harder and harder to hold it back.

He only hits her once, and not in front of Sidney. But that once is enough for her to leave him, though he swears he'll never do it again, and when she leaves, the rage only grows, sharp-toothed and about to consume him.

He needs an outlet for it. A true outlet, one that's not picking fights with his wife, especially now that she's left him.

And one day he finds one. He's left Sidney with his sister and gone for a drive, just to clear his head. That's when he sees her. Lauren O'Malley with her broken-down car. He doesn't know her name, of course, but it's a fucking sign from the universe, isn't it?

She doesn't look like Julie. That doesn't matter. He can tell by the state of the car, older than his, that no one will miss her for a few hours at least.

She smiles at him when she gets in. The audacity. He could be anyone, shouldn't she know better?

He'll raise Sidney to know better.

Almost a week after the third one, he decides then and there he is going to stop. He'll give himself one night, a few hours at the shack where he's been taking them to shave their heads, the one the cops haven't found, rotting and half covered in kudzu. One night to make sure all the evidence is gone, nothing to tie the girls back to him, and then he'll be done. He'll leave Sidney with his sister again; say he's going out on a date, trying to get back out there. He'll buy a bottle of women's perfume from the Rite Aid and spritz it on before he comes back so she believes him.

But the more he thinks about it, the more he doesn't want to call his sister, his sister who lives an hour away and has two kids of her own. Her husband died. His wife left. She gets sympathy and he gets knowing looks from the women in the grocery store like they were just counting the days until Julie left him.

Her husband died drunk driving, though; what does that say?

No. He's not going to leave Sidney with his sister. He's not going to ask his sister for help. He can do this himself, like everything else. He hires a babysitter, some local girl from the high school who's put flyers up. He tells her he's got a date, asks if she can watch his daughter for a few hours. She agrees.

The babysitter shows up a half hour late, apologizing like that's going to make any difference. He just nods and leaves, but in the car on the way to the lake he feels the rage bubble up again.

He thought this would quiet it. Tonight was supposed to quiet it for good. But all he can think about is the apologetic look on the babysitter's face, like her apologies actually mean a damn. It's the same thing his sisters would do, Julie would do—completely screw him over and act like an apology was going to make it better.

He knows, then, that the rage will not rest until he kills this girl, too.

But not tonight. If he does it tonight they'll know it's him. He has to wait.

He tells the rage to be patient, and that quiets it enough—that and the sight of the shack, and the lake where he's dumped the girls. He's got it down to a science almost, an exact series of steps that soothes the rage enough that he can go on throughout his day.

He picks them up. Sometimes it's easy, sometimes he has an excuse, like for the one in the neighborhood. Other times he just takes them—he's skinny but he's tall, and the chloroform-soaked rag helps knock them out, like it did for the one he grabbed from the Piggly Wiggly parking lot. His second.

He didn't like doing it that way. He prefers when they come willingly, when he doesn't have to resort to drugging them. Prefers it because there's something about watching the panic on their faces when he drives them out to the lake. He can pinpoint almost the exact moment that it happens, when their suspicion turns to fear.

It'll be even more satisfying with this one. The babysitter. He knows he should stop at three, but he also knows the rage will never leave him, and he never wants to show that rage to Sidney, so he has to.

He has to kill this one. He had to kill all of them, because otherwise this rage, this thing that made his wife leave him, would show itself to Sidney, and he can't have that.

Really, he tells himself, he's doing this for her.

Chapter Fifteen

WHEN HE'S finished, I can't breathe. He says it all so dispassionately, the most words he's ever spoken to me since he was arrested five years ago. Even ten minutes after we've hung up, I'm still standing there, the phone in my hand, staring down at it. It's what I cannot get out of my head. He did this for me.

I was doing it for you.

All along. All along, it has been my fault. It has always been because of me.

The girls are dead because of me.

LAUREN O'MALLEY
ALICIA GRAVES
MELISSA WAGNER
DAWN SCHAEFER
SAMANTHA MARKHAM
JUNE HARGROVE

SAVANNAH BAUNACH
LILAH CRENSHAW

They are dead because of ~~my father~~ me.

I vomit. Right into the bushes.

But at least I know where the girls are being taken. The shack. I don't know where it is, though, so I don't know how I'll be able to get there in time.

I should just go to the sheriff, shouldn't I? I should just go tell him right now to check the shack in the woods for his daughter, for Mavis, for whoever's doing this.

I find the number for the sheriff's office online easily enough. But no one picks up when I call, so I try again. And again. I try the investigations department, even, but no one picks up there, either.

I try to call Mavis one more time, because I need to hear her voice. I need to hear that she's okay. Need to tell her that I need her help. Need her back. She's not the final target. I am.

She still doesn't answer, and I swear before catching myself.

I need to go find Sally Louise. I need to save her, and if Mavis won't help, then I need to do it alone, because if I don't I'm afraid all I'll become is just like Dad.

I bike home faster than I ever have in my life, nearly wiping out twice on gravel roads leading to our trailer. I will not get to the lake in time at this point, and I don't know how much longer Sally Louise has—or if she's already dead.

Gram is home when I'm there, and I run in.

"I need to borrow the car," I say.

"You ain't got a license. Where're you going?"

"Friend's house," I say. She turns and looks at me, takes in how out of breath I am, how disheveled. "Please, Gram," I add, desperate. "I don't have time to explain."

She studies me for a long moment, and I realize if she says no, I'll just take the keys and go, anyway, and deal with the consequences later. I'm already halfway to them when she shrugs and turns back to the TV like she really doesn't want to know, and I send up a silent thank you to whoever the fuck is watching that something, for once, is going right.

It takes me two tries to start the car, my hands are shaking so badly. But I finally manage to, and nearly take out a tree reversing out of our drive, my foot is so heavy on the gas. I floor it down the back road that leads away from our trailer. Gram's car is older than Mavis's, and it takes me miles to truly get the hang of the pressure I need to put on the gas.

I drive down to the entrance to the park by Cardinal Lake. I don't have a clue where to find the old shack that my dad mentioned. Driving around the woods would take hours, hours I know Sally doesn't have.

"Shit," I curse, hitting my fists on the steering wheel. "Shit, shit shit." Why didn't I ask him? Why didn't I fucking ask him where the shack was? Why didn't I get him to tell me?

But he was able to drive them out there. He was able to dump their bodies into the lake. There's no real roads back here, but if I can just drive fast enough, if I can find where Sally is, then—

Maybe I can find her before it's too late.

I push harder on the gas and drive into the woods, not on a walking trail, hoping for one wild second that June or Savannah or even fucking Lilah will show up, will show me where they died, but right when I want them to bother me they've vanished, and the only thing haunting me now is the possibility that I might not get to Sally Louise in time and she might turn into another ghost that will never let me go.

My foot is heavy on the brake as I maneuver the car through the path in the woods, stopping every few seconds to look around. This car wasn't made to be off-road, but I can't think about all the damage I'm causing to it or how much it's going to cost to fix it.

Every once in a while I look down at my phone. There's no service out here, yet I find myself desperately checking the time, or to see if Mavis has called, or sent a message, or something that indicates she's just mad at me, that she's not—

No. I can't think that. I am looking for Sally Louise, and Mavis has not texted because she's angry with me. He hasn't gotten her. He hasn't. That wouldn't make sense.

I drive faster. The path is clear enough that the car fits, so I accelerate, just a little more, just so I can hurry.

And then out of nowhere a tree rises up out of the ground, one I swear wasn't there before, and it's too late to stop and I can't remember where the brake is and in my panic punch the gas down harder.

I close my eyes and brace for impact, and then everything goes black.

Chapter Sixteen

I WAKE up with my head pounding and the dawning horror creeping in that I have no idea where I am—and that I'm not alone.

I'm not in the car. The last thing I remember was being in the car . . . and now?

Now I'm in the woods. I open my eyes, blink a few times to clear the blurriness, and then realize—

I'm in the shack. It's barely a standing structure now, just rotting planks and kudzu, and a door that's almost fallen off its hinges. As my eyes adjust, I look around in horror.

There, next to me, is Mavis. Her eyes are closed, and for a second I can't breathe because all I can think is, *She's dead she's dead she's dead,* but then I see the rise and fall of her chest, and I breathe a sigh of relief.

She's alive. Oh god, she's alive and she's here which means—which means—

I'm not the final victim.

She is.

I'm just here to watch.

I do start screaming then, not caring who's hearing or if he comes back or—

"Shut up."

I turn. Sally Louise sits next to me, tired and ragged. There's a cut under her left eye. Half of her head—

Is shaved.

Oh god.

"Are you a ghost?" I choke out, before she reaches out and slaps a hand over my mouth, solid and clammy and real and I almost have to laugh.

"Clearly not," she hisses. "Now shut up, or he's going to come back."

I nod, and she removes her hand from my mouth. I want to ask her why she's here, why she hasn't tried to leave or run, but my mouth feels fuzzy and my head can't form the words. She seems to guess at it, though, because I follow her gaze down to her ankle, which is swollen and purple.

"I think it's broken," she says quietly. "I tried to run, and he—he caught me and . . ." She grimaces.

I shudder.

"Who is he?" I ask, because I can at least get those words out. She shakes her head.

"I have no fucking idea, Sid."

"Where—we should go. We should leave—"

"How? Your girlfriend's unconscious, I can't move, and I'm pretty sure if you tried to stand now you'd fall on your ass." She shakes her head. "We're stuck here until he kills us."

She sounds so final about it.

"Sally, I'm sorry—"

"For what? You didn't kidnap me," she says, and I shake my head so fast it makes me feel nauseous. She doesn't get it. I'm still responsible.

I'm about to tell her that when the door to the shack creaks open and we both fall silent. Sally closes her eyes and slumps against the wall immediately, but I don't react fast enough, because I lock eyes with a man as soon as the door opens.

I don't know him. It's not Terry, or Johnny, and I'm momentarily comforted by that before I'm absolutely terrified by it. He's tall, lanky, but with the build of someone who either works out or has a physical job. He's white, almost ghostly pale. Blond. I don't know him. I've never seen him.

But then he speaks. His voice is scratchy, somewhat high, and I realize then, horribly, that I know it.

Jeremy Schaefer. Dawn's brother.

He must see the recognition on my face because he smiles then, and the sight of it makes me want to throw up.

"So you did figure it out," he says, and steps inside, shutting the door behind him. His voice hasn't changed in the four years since he recorded the podcast. "I knew you would. It's why I changed up the schedule."

"I didn't," I whisper. "I didn't, not—not until now."

He cocks his head. "I thought you'd be a better detective than that, little Sidney. Or didn't you go ask your daddy for help? I'm surprised you didn't find me sooner, all things considered. Then again, I tried not to be as predictable as he was."

He crouches down so he's nearly eye level with me, and I flinch away.

"Oh, you're braver than that," he says. He nudges Mavis with the toe of his boot. She doesn't stir. "Runnin' all over town tryin' to catch me, draggin' your little girl along with you? I was going to wait until the date my sister died to kill you. But then you had to involve your little girlfriend, and I realized you were getting too close, that I needed you out of my way. You even recruited the sheriff's daughter. I didn't plan on killing her—you were supposed to be my last, I think you know that. But I think this is gonna be so much better, don't you?" He stands up, and without warning, aims a kick at Sally's ankle. She screams, and in the second she does, Mavis's eyes fly open.

"Mavis," I croak, my mouth dry, and Jeremy laughs, louder even than Sally Louise's continued screaming.

"I want you to tell me, Sid," Jeremy says at last, once the sound has finally died down, "why I did it. It's the question that's been eating at you from the inside, every day. I know, because it's been eating at me. Why did your dad do this? Why did these girls deserve to die?" He smiles again. "Why are the sheriff's daughter and your little girlfriend about to die instead of you?"

"I don't—I don't—"

"I think you do," he says. "Come on now."

I grit my teeth. It's one thing to tell Sally Louise I'm responsible, to know ~~someone~~ Jeremy did this because of Dad. It's another thing entirely to admit that to him.

"This is my fault."

"Go on."

"You're . . ." I struggle to speak. My tongue feels heavy in my mouth. "You're going to kill me."

"Good guess, but not quite. Try again."

"You're . . . you're going to kill Sally Louise," I say. "And . . . and Mavis?"

"Why?"

I think about what Dad said about sending a message, and it finally clicks. "You're going to frame me for this."

"Bingo, kiddo," he says. His voice finally hardens. "Your daddy didn't get the death penalty, but maybe you will. This town ain't gonna like someone murdering their girls twice, especially not another Crane. So." He smiles. "Which one should I start with first? You can choose."

I can't breathe.

"Dawn—Dawn wouldn't have—"

"Don't you *dare* tell me what my sister would have wanted, Sidney Crane," he spits. "Don't you dare act like you know what I'm going through. It was enough of an insult to get your fucking little email talking about sympathy and how my sister should still be here. You think I don't know that?"

"Jeremy . . ."

"Shut *up*," he snaps, and this time he lunges for Mavis. I try to stop him, but I'm too slow, too clumsy, can't get my body there in time. Mavis screams at the same time Jeremy grabs her wrist and yanks her to her feet.

"Choose," he says again. "Which girl do you want to see die first? What's your final order going to be, huh?"

JUNE HARGROVE
SAVANNAH BAUNACH
LILAH CRENSHAW

JUNE HARGROVE
SAVANNAH BAUNACH
LILAH CRENSHAW
MAVIS—

"I'm sorry," I choke out. "I'm sorry about Dawn, Jeremy, but this won't bring her back—"

"I'm not trying to bring her back," he says. "I'm trying to make you suffer." He tightens his arm around Mavis's neck, and she whimpers, her fingernails clawing into his arm, desperately trying to push him away.

I don't know what to do. I can feel that panic clouding over me, and I fight to stay where I am.

"Decide," he says again. "Which one's going first?"

I swallow. Sally Louise catches my eye. I have no idea what to do, how this is going to end. If any of us are going to get out of here alive.

"I don't want to," I say, just to have something to say, and Jeremy's face twists.

"That's not how this goes," he says. "You have to decide." As he speaks, he loosens his grip on Mavis just slightly.

She makes eye contact with me.

"Keep him talking," she mouths, and I scramble around in my brain for something to say.

"How?" I ask. "Tell me—tell me how I'm going to kill them. You owe me that, at least. If I'm being framed."

Jeremy smiles. "You already know how you're going to, Sid. Just like your dad. Like it's personal."

"You think I'm strong enough to strangle someone?" I ask. "They'll notice. They'll figure out that they're different from the others."

Jeremy laughs. "Cops around here ain't that smart," he says. His arm loosens a little more. Beside me, Sally grimaces, but I watch as she shifts, just a little.

Think, Sid. Think.

We're in a shack that's falling apart. There has to be something in here I can grab, something I can use as a weapon.

But I need to keep Jeremy talking while I do.

"It was stupid of you," I say, trying a different tactic. "Kidnapping the sheriff's daughter. You think he won't notice she's missing?"

Sally Louise nods encouragingly. Jeremy sneers.

"You think I'm that dumb? I threw her phone out at the gas station. Those pricks who own it can take the heat for a little while I finish up here. Trash like you. We thought it was Johnny for the longest time, you know? Apparently he and Dawn were dating, which nearly broke my mama's heart when she found out. I thought about pinning this on him, but that would mean you don't suffer, and that's really what I want." He smiles. "I'm sure the sheriff and his good old boys will come find you, but you and I both know how long it took them to catch your daddy. He won't be fast enough this time, even if it is his own daughter."

Sally's teeth have dug into her lip so hard she's drawn blood. But the only person Jeremy is focused on right now is me.

Good. If I can keep him that way, then maybe . . . maybe we might have a chance. If we can just get him down, knock him out—he's strong but maybe he's not fast.

"You—you can't make me do it," I say. "Kill them."

"You think I can't?" he asks. "Or I can just kill them and make you watch. I killed those other three girls, didn't I?"

"Killed them in the same way my dad killed your sister?" I ask, and his face contorts.

"They're nothing like my sister," he says. "My sister fought back. My sister almost got away, is what we heard at the sentencing. You didn't know that, did you? He breathed in too much chloroform and knocked himself out and she almost got away." He's breathing harder now. Sally Louise starts to push herself up, but his attention is solely on me. "Do you know what else I found out that day, too? My sister is dead because of you. He said he wouldn't have picked her except she babysat you once. You probably don't even remember."

"I don't," I say quietly. "I'm sorry, I don't remember—"

"She's dead because of you!" he yells, and at the same time Mavis yells *"Now!"* and Sally Louise lunges at Jeremy with a piece of rotten wood. All three of them go toppling out of the shed, the back of it breaking underneath them, and I scream, stumbling after them just as the structure gives way, landing hard on the ground. I push myself up and nearly topple over again, before grabbing another rotten plank and steadying myself. Mavis has landed on Jeremy, but he's flailing under her, Sally desperately trying to pin one of his legs down, but neither of them is strong enough and he's almost sitting up.

"Bitch," he snarls as he flails, his elbow slamming into Mavis's nose, and she screams, blood pouring out of it. I stagger to my feet, clutching the wooden plank.

"Sid!" Sally yells, and I take the plank and raise it over my head, praying I hit Jeremy and not Mavis, bringing it down on his face with such force I hear the crack of cartilage underneath it, but all I can think is—

I don't want to kill him. I don't want to kill him. I don't want to kill him.

But I don't want him to hurt us anymore.

Jeremy roars, clutching at his face with one hand. He's finally twisted so Mavis is off him, and with his free hand he shoves Sally away, who lands on her ankle with a yelp. His eyes fix on me, and the next thing I notice I'm staring down the barrel of a pistol.

"I didn't want to do it this way," he pants. Blood pours out of his nose and his voice is slightly muffled, but his movements are sure. "It's so messy. It's not satisfying. Your father took his damn time killing each girl so they suffered, so they felt it. It's not fair these ones are going to die quickly." He points the gun at Sally, then swings it to Mavis.

"I told you to pick, Sid," he says. "Pick. We ain't got all day."

"Jeremy, please—"

He swings it to me. "Or I can just kill you instead if you don't choose. How about that? Do you think your daddy will be sad if something happens to you?"

If this is someone's idea of revenge, if I'm the last one—would it even make a difference to you?

"I'll count backward from five. Five."

Lauren O'Malley.

"Four."

Alicia Graves.

"Three."

Melissa Wagner.

"Two."

Dawn Schaefer.

"One."

Samantha Markham.

There is a sound. A loud one. There is Jeremy, yelling, and then falling—or maybe he's pushed, because for a split second all I see is a flash of shaved head. A girl turns, and I know her. It's Dawn.

No.

It's June. Lauren. Lilah. Alicia. Samantha. A girl, her features morphing and shifting. June Savannah Lilah June Lauren Alicia DawnJuneAliciaDawnLilahDawnJuneSamanthaMelissa and I see her, I see her, I see her.

And then she's gone, and I just see Mavis and Sally, all of us looking at Jeremy, blood pooling under his head.

"Is he . . ."

But none of us wants to say it.

"Did you . . . did you see . . ."

None of us wants to answer that, either.

"The gun misfired," Sally says suddenly, confidently. "Right? He—he was going to shoot us and the gun misfired and he fell and hit his head—"

"That's what happened," Mavis says shakily, and they both look to me for confirmation.

"Yes," I say woodenly, even as I am still staring at the girl, the ghost, even as we all are. "That's what happened."

It's the last thing I say before my vision starts to blur and I feel myself starting to fall and then for the second time that day, the world goes dark.

Chapter Seventeen

WHEN I wake up, I'm surrounded by white, and for a second I think maybe I am in prison. Or maybe the gun didn't misfire, maybe I'm dead, and it's just this blank white nothingness for eternity.

But no. I'm not. I smell something chemical, and I know I'm in a hospital.

"Careful."

I know that voice.

"Gram?"

"Don't sit up too fast," she says, and then she's there, holding my hand, smelling again like cigarettes and White Diamonds. She must've just come back from a smoke break. I wonder how long I've been out.

The room slowly comes back into focus. Across from me is Mavis, two people who look almost identical to her hovering over her bed. *Her parents,* I think, though I realize I've never met them.

Next to her is Sally Louise. Her ankle is propped up. Sheriff Kepler is nowhere to be seen. They both look like they've been awake far longer than I have.

"How long—"

"Just an hour," Sally answers, sounding almost bored. "You didn't even wake up when they packed you in the ambulance."

An ambulance? There was an ambulance?

How did we get found? How did we get out of the woods?

"I—"

"Easy," Gram says, and it's then that I wonder how she even got to the hospital, since as far as I know her car is still somewhere in the woods. "You'll get your questions answered. And I think the sheriff has several for you, as well."

I groan and lie down, close my eyes. I can't bring myself to open them again, and before I know it I've fallen back into a dreamless sleep.

When I wake, it's dark outside. Gram is gone. The room is quiet. Across from me, Mavis is flipping through a battered copy of *Jane Eyre*. Sally Louise is nowhere to be seen.

I mumble something, and Mavis looks at me.

"Hey," she says quietly. It's the first thing we've really spoken to each other since the shack. Since our fight. "You're up again."

"Barely," I say, and she smiles. "You okay?"

"Fine. Just a concussion. Bruised ribs. Busted nose. I'll be okay," she says. She closes her eyes briefly. "Sid, about—about our fight."

"It's fine," I say. I take a breath. "You're right. I'm not my dad."

Mavis looks uncomfortable "I shouldn't have said that."

"No, you're right. Someone needed to say it." Her face softens. "And you aren't your sister. Even if . . . even if your parents wish you were."

Mavis swallows. A wound for a wound. I look at her and all I can see is all the ways we have hurt each other, all the ways we can hurt each other, our own ghosts surrounding us and refusing to let us go.

"I can apologize for you being in this mess, though," I say. "If it weren't for me, Jeremy wouldn't have—wouldn't have taken you."

"That's his fault," she says. She pushes herself out of bed and crosses over to me. "You know that, right? Jeremy doing what he did—killing June and Savannah and Lilah—he might say it's because of you, your dad might say it's because of you, but at the end of the day they're the ones who did it. It isn't your fault."

"My dad told me," I say flatly, "that he did it to . . . to protect me from him. So he'd have another outlet for his—rage." The sob I've been holding in since I was thirteen finally comes pouring out, and I look up at Mavis. "And I believe him, Mavis.

Him, Jeremy . . . I—I know you told me I'm not my dad and I believe you, but he killed Dawn because of *me*. June and Savannah and Lilah are dead because of *me*."

"Sid . . . ," she says, and then she's sitting on my bed, her arms around me, and I let myself lean into her touch and sob into her shoulder. "Sid. It's not your fault. You are not responsible for what your dad or Jeremy did. Okay? Just like—just like I'm not responsible for Ginny going missing." She rubs my back. "Or Sally's not responsible for what her father does. It's not our job to atone for what they did."

But it is. It is. It has to be, or I've been chasing these ghosts for nothing. I've been haunted for nothing.

I ask Mavis what I could not ask back in the forest, by the lake.

"Is Jeremy dead?" I whisper. "Did we—"

"The gun misfired," Mavis says simply. "He's dead." She pulls back and looks at me. "That's what Sally told the sheriff. That's what we'll both say, when they ask. The gun misfired. He got blown back by the force of it, and he fell and hit his head and he's dead."

"You saw them, too," I say. "You saw them."

"Them?" Now Mavis looks confused. "No, Sid. No. I just saw you. He had the gun pointed right at you, and you stepped toward him, and you were reaching for it when it fired and then he started to fall and you—your arms were out like you'd pushed him and . . . he fell," she finishes. "He fell."

I didn't want to kill him. I didn't.

But maybe I did.

"I'm not . . . I'm not a killer," I say desperately, babbling now, and Mavis takes my face in her hands and looks at me.

"You're not a killer," she says firmly. "You're not your dad. Jeremy Schaefer fell and hit his head because he was trying to kill us. Trying to kill *you*. That's the end of it."

She pulls me to her and I take a breath, because she is holding me and that feels right, and I didn't want to kill Jeremy Schaefer. I didn't.

I didn't.

I did.

Sheriff Kepler looks like he's aged thirty years in the past week. We're back in that same small room. He has a folder spread out in front of him, a folder about what happened to all the other girls, to us, to me.

He knows I did not do it. I think.

SHERIFF KEPLER: This is just a formality. I hate having you in here, despite what you may think.

SID: I know. How's Sally?

SHERIFF KEPLER: Faster on crutches than I am on two feet. How's Marybeth?

SID: Fine. Johnny's at the house watching

her, I think. She doesn't wanna be alone.

SHERIFF KEPLER: Huh. *[Clears throat.]* Now. Sid. I've already heard from the Hastings girl and from Sally, but I want to get a final statement from you just so we can go ahead and close the book on this. No one in this town wants any of this dragged out.

SID: I understand.

SHERIFF KEPLER: Good. Tell me what happened after you woke up in the shack.

SID: There was . . . this guy. Jeremy Schaefer. I didn't recognize him until he spoke—I knew his voice from that . . . from that podcast he did on his sister disappearing.

SHERIFF KEPLER: *Dawn of Justice*. My wife was obsessed with it when it came out.

SID: Yeah. And he—he started talking about . . . about killing the other girls, about how he wanted to kill me but it was better if he killed Mavis and Sally and framed me for it, because then I—then I would suffer like he had. He grabbed Mavis, and then . . .

SHERIFF KEPLER: And then what?

SID: Mavis told me to keep him talking so that he was distracted. He had his arm around her neck and he loosened it when he was talking. So I asked him about the girls, and his sister, and he said—he said she was dead because of me. Because my father had decided to kill her after she babysat me.

SHERIFF KEPLER: The transcript from the sentencing confirms your father said that, yes.

SID: Yeah, so . . . he started yelling then. About how Dawn was dead because of me. And then Mavis was yelling and we charged him and landed outside and then he hit Mavis, and I hit him with a plank and then he was starting to get up and he—he had a gun. And he said I needed to choose which one of them was going to die first. And if I didn't choose, it was going to be me.

SHERIFF KEPLER: And then what happened?

SID: The gun misfired, I think. But the force knocked him back and he fell and hit his head and then he wasn't moving and I . . . I blacked out.

[Beat.]

SHERIFF KEPLER: That's it?

SID: That's it.

SHERIFF KEPLER: Is there anything else you can tell me, any more information you might be able to give?

SID: No.

SHERIFF KEPLER: I see. Well. Your statement goes with what the other girls have said, so I think it's safe to say we can call this an accident.

He stands, the interview clearly over. I do, too, and the sheriff looks at me for a long moment.

"Off the record," he says. "One less freak like Jeremy Schaefer in the world, the better."

"Of course," I say. He wants this done as badly as I do, I know. The rest of this town needs to move on. But he stops me right as he's about to open the door.

"There's going to be a memorial for the girls," he says.

"I know," I say. The news had mentioned the memorial the other night.

"Not just . . . not just the girls this year," he says meaningfully. "It's been ten years since—well. You know."

"I know," I say.

"I think it would be best . . ."

"You don't want me to go." I take a breath to try and steady myself. After everything. After *everything*, no one can look at me without seeing my father.

Jeremy got what he wanted.

"I think, Sid, this town needs to move on. And you being there would just remind them of the fact that they can't."

Again I think of what Sally said when I mentioned reaching out to the families of Dad's victims. This time, though, I have a response.

"What about me?" I ask. "Don't I get to move on?"

Sheriff Kepler gives me a long look, but he doesn't answer my question. He just leaves me standing there in that back room like I'm thirteen years old again, still in the shadow of what my dad has done.

The memorial is out by the gazebo in the town square, in the same place they held the meeting before the search for Savannah.

I stand at the back. I'm not supposed to be there, and if anyone looks too long, they'll know it's me. The murderer's kid.

But this time, I'm not alone. Mavis and Sally stand with me. Mavis's hand is interlaced with mine; Sally is leaning heavily on her crutches. The three of us are far enough away that no one is even looking at us. We look like just another group of teenagers attending the memorial for girls they knew.

Jenny, Savannah's younger sister, stands up at the podium. Sheriff Kepler is up there too, dressed in his full uniform. Beside him are the families of each of the other girls—the families they could still find. The ones that didn't move away or leave or shut themselves off from the rest of us like they have the right to do.

"I . . . I want to say a few words about my sister, but first, I want to read out the names of—of all the girls who went missing or were murdered in this town," Jenny says shakily.

I close my eyes as she reads the names. I already know them by heart.

LAUREN O'MALLEY
ALICIA GRAVES
MELISSA WAGNER
DAWN SCHAEFER
SAMANTHA MARKHAM
JUNE HARGROVE
SAVANNAH BAUNACH
LILAH CRENSHAW

At Lilah's name, Sally Louise starts quietly sobbing, and I hold her close to me as best I can. We watch as the girl pulls out a lighter and lights a candle, and all in front of us, people light some of their own—those little white ones we'd get at church during Christmas that drip wax on your hand even through the paper shield.

The town mourns together, and Mavis, Sally, and I cling to each other, thinking of these girls whose lives were cut too short, girls who begged to be seen and the wrong person answered. Girls who didn't deserve to die like they did. Girls turned into a billboard or a poster begging someone to just see them after death, too.

Girls my father killed. Girls my father killed whose deaths I had nothing to do with, but their ghosts had forced me to see them anyway, to witness them, because someone had to, because no one else would.

I clutch Mavis and Sally to me, and I know then, as everyone in front of us blows out their candles, that the girls will not come to visit me anymore.

"Let's go," Mavis whispers, and the three of us walk/hobble away, back to Mavis's car, off to do our own memorial. We are going to drive out to Cardinal Lake, set fire to as much of the shack as we can. Sally was a Girl Scout; she says she knows how, and I believe her. I am going to hold on to these girls that are alive, pay my respects to the ones that are dead, and try my hardest to believe that they aren't dead because of me.

I'm not going to let them haunt me anymore.

ACKNOWLEDGMENTS

I'VE BEEN working on *Have You Seen This Girl* on and off since 2018, and the people I could thank since then would fill a whole book by themselves. This book was the hardest I've ever written for a myriad of reasons, and I'm so grateful to everyone listed here for their help in making it a reality.

First, to Eric Smith, whose enthusiasm for this book knows no bounds, for not batting an eye when I switched genres (again). None of my books would exist without your passion and dedication, and I'm forever grateful.

Stephanie Stein, Sophie Schmidt, and Sara Schonfeld: Thank you all for your insight, notes, GIF reactions, and editorial wisdom. You helped make this book sadder, scarier, and more layered than it would have been without you. And thank you for your patience—I think I finally got the timeline of Sid's story right after a whole year.

To the team at HarperTeen, including Mark Rifkin,

Annabelle Sinoff, Nicole Moulaison, Shannon Cox, and Lauren Levite. Special shout-out to Shona McCarthy, Laaren Brown, and Lisa Lester Kelly, my production editor, copy editor, and proofreader, for making sure that the timeline of the missing girls actually made sense. Thank you for letting me stet all of my dialect and weird formatting choices.

To Toma Vagner and Julia Feingold for the absolutely striking cover. Y'all knocked it out of the park. It truly is a work of art and captures the atmosphere of Sid's story in a way I couldn't have even imagined.

To my parents for the support, for talking up my books at your book club, and for always asking "How's the writing going?" even if the answer is sometimes "Not great!" One of these days, I'll write a book where the parents are as loving and supportive as y'all. (It isn't this one.)

I submitted a draft of *Have You Seen This Girl* to the Tin House YA Workshop in 2021, and the feedback and excitement there was invaluable. Special thanks to Mark Oshiro, Maya Gittelman, Trang Thanh Tran, and all of the "Meat Cutes."

Writing a book often feels like a solitary process, but friends make it easier, and I'm so lucky that I have so many in my life. Bree, Casek, Geertje, Jean, Kadan, Kath, Olivia, Nell, Rae, and Sneha—thank you. To writer friends Camryn Garrett, Marieke Nijkamp, Corinne Duyvis, Dante Medema, and Rey Noble, thank you all for keeping me sane during the process of writing and publishing a book.

Jon/Fine, Cate, and Valeria for the love and friendship across oceans and time zones. Love is stored in asking "Okay, but why are you AWAKE."

Sarah and Alec for the unending support, for giving my books to your students, for the snacks, the hangouts, the book recs, and the absolute shenanigans. I love y'all and you're my favorites, and we know this is true because I always roll nat 1s on deception checks.

Erica and Carolyn: I don't even know how to thank y'all except to say I love you.

To my own Granny, who so much of Gram is based on: I would not be who I am today without your love. I love you to the moon and back.

I first got the idea for this book in 2018 listening to a true crime podcast and driving down I-40 with my best friend. Kate, you are everything anyone could ever ask for in a best friend. I'll sing Reba with you and talk about dialect any time.

Writing a character who shares your identity always feels like exposing a raw nerve, and I would not have had the courage to write Sid without all the queer and trans writers who have come before me and shared their stories.

To my readers: Thank you for loving all my messy, complicated characters and following me across genres. It's because of y'all I get to keep writing books, and that means the world.

And finally, as always, to Hannah for letting me talk through all the tricky aspects of this book, for supplying me with little treats on deadline, for letting me ramble to you about specific laws in North Carolina and my Notion setup for the outline, and for a million other things. I love you.